OUR LADY OF THE SNOWS

Other books by Morley Callaghan:

Strange Fugitive (1928)
An Autumn Penitent (1929)
A Native Argosy (1929)
It's Never Over (1930)
Broken Journey (1932)
Such Is My Beloved (1934)
They Shall Inherit the Earth (1935)
Now That April's Here (1936)
More Joy in Heaven (1937)
The Varsity Story (1945)
Luke Baldwin's Vow (1949)
The Loved and the Lost (1951)
The Many Colored Coat (1960)
A Passion in Rome (1961)
That Summer in Paris (1963)
A Fine and Private Place (1975)
Close to the Sun Again (1977)
A Time for Judas (1983)

Morley Callaghan

OUR LADY OF THE SNOWS

St. Martin's Press
New York

Library of Congress Cataloging in Publication Data

Callaghan, Morley, 1903–
    Our lady of the snows.

    I. Title.
PR9199.3.C2709   1986   813'.52   85-25059
ISBN 0-312-59054-7

First published in Canada by Macmillan of Canada.

First U.S. Edition

10   9   8   7   6   5   4   3   2   1

For Mischi, Brendan, and Darcy

OUR LADY OF THE SNOWS

1

THERE HAD BEEN NO SNOW, NONE AT ALL, AND THEN on Christmas Eve around nine snow started falling in big wet flakes that quickly melted in the mild air. The snow came from over the lake, moving east for miles along the lake front, and then the fall grew heavier till the downtown cluster of great towers, layers of light in the darkness, turned golden in the shimmering veil of snow, and to the east, ten blocks from the towers, the snow fell on an old dilapidated neighborhood of rundown houses and small stores. Everything in the neighborhood looked better in the snow. But that four-storeyed hotel on the corner, the Bradley House, did not need the snow. It was of brick, always freshly painted white, with floodlights on all sides concealed under the eaves. The entrance to the big lounge faced a lot used for parking cars across the street. Around the corner, the hotel had another face. Flagstone steps led to two Corinthian white pillars and a black door, making a handsome entrance to three upstairs apartments, and to Mr. Gilhooley's. The discreet electric sign, "Bar", was to the left of the door. The last of the Bradleys, J.C., who was rich and owned horses, lived in one of the fine apartments with the two pretty young Stenson sisters, who rode and had won many ribbons at horse shows.

As yet there was no snow on the ground; it kept melting. Under the lights the whole white brick hotel began to gleam. A big doorman in a blue-and-red uniform was hurrying to open a taxi door. Neighbors straggled along the street to the lounge. Two big men in windbreakers, caps, and old pants kept looking up at the sky. "Well, what do you know," said one happily, "a white Christmas after all. My kid'll like this." To the left of the lounge entrance and away from its neon light, a bundled-up bag lady, clutching the plastic bag tied with cord that held all she owned, was looking at the sky. The wet cold nights were coming on. The nights for sleeping in doorways were over. A kid dragging a small Christmas tree along the pavement accidentally swung the tree, almost knocking the bag lady to the ground. He looked back furtively, then started to run with the tree as if he had stolen it. The woman stared across the street at the car park. She would sleep in the old car with flat tires near the back fence tonight.

In the snow, the hotel took on a silvery sheen, then gradually under the floodlights it became a glowing giant ice crystal with strange fiery lights in it, a magic crystal set down in the dark shabby neighborhood. Yet even in the old days, in fact ever since the first eccentric Bradley had built the hotel eighty years ago, it had been freshly painted and always white, and in the summer time brightly lit; it kept its own magic glow as the neighborhood deteriorated. Anyone born in the vicinity, whose family, prospering, had moved north, remembered the Bradley and what the sight of it had meant to them.

Gil Gilhooley, the bartender, the son of a local barber, had always remembered this hotel wherever he went. First, of course, he had gone to the university, having won scholarships in English and history. Then, wanting to see the world and travel and write, he had learned the bartender's trade. But whether he worked in Chicago, Los Angeles, or Las Vegas, he remembered the Bradley, the clean, bright meeting place that always prospered, and he came home and did a deal with the last of the Bradleys. They set up the great mahogany bar—Mr. Gilhooley's—for uptown people who could believe they were slumming in comfort in sophisticated company yet within earshot of a colorful tribal gathering in the Bradley lounge. Now its fame as a meeting place had spread across the city. Not the bar, but the lounge. When the Montreal gangster Julius Shapiro was found brutally beaten and dead in his car miles away on the highway, his wife had revealed to the police that he had gone out to meet someone at the Bradley lounge. Two months earlier, there had been a story in the papers that Manny Schultz, a Brooklyn drug dealer found with his throat cut in a gutter near the airport, had left word with a friend that he had an appointment in the Bradley lounge. Johnny Rocco, found dead, packed in the trunk of his car among boxes from an exclusive women's-wear store, had been last seen drinking with a stranger in the Bradley lounge.

But these stories couldn't give the Bradley a bad name. It was too peaceful a place, too like a family club, to nurture such violence, those who knew it said. There was never any brawling in the Bradley and never a killing, and certainly never a police raid. Even the lounge prostitutes who sat at tables called "the block" respected the law, for they never solicited a John and never took one to a room in the hotel. They used the old tourist house up the street, where they registered legally. Any man could feel secure in the lounge as long as he was quiet and behaved himself. Even undercover policemen with hidden cameras felt at home there.

But as a result of the stories, Mr. Gilhooley's, with its side-street entrance, its big doorman, and its air of distinction, became even more fashionable. Even tonight, in the snow on Christmas Eve, the regulars kept coming in. Many cars were parked along the side street. Joe, the doorman, his shoulders covered with snow, kept calling out cheerfully "Merry Christmas" as he opened each taxi door, and across the road, in the street light, five children led by a stout woman in a fur coat were singing a Christmas carol as the young lawyer, Swanson, from the prestigious firm of Wakefield and Wright, came in. Mr. Justice Gibbons, a stout man of sixty, hatless, with thick silvery hair and a noble head, followed.

Tonight the Judge was a lonely, troubled man, and in Gil he had a sympathetic and literate friend. Yesterday, the Judge's name had been in all the papers. A young woman had charged her lover with a brutal assault, and then in court had refused to give evidence against him. This was contempt for the law, the Judge said: it was contempt of court, and he sentenced her to thirty days in jail. The victim was in jail, the criminal free, and there was a terrible outcry that would have shaken any judge's confidence. But these days the Judge was not sure of himself. Bad things had happened to him. His wife, whom he used to wheel around his neighborhood, so crippled with arthritis, was now in a nursing home. But a month earlier she had insisted he get rid of his dog.

Why this had happened was a story, and he wanted to tell it to Gil, but first the Judge had to see Bradley, because it was Christmas Eve, see him before he went down to the bar. He had been the Bradley family lawyer until appointed to the bench. Tonight, as usual, he would sit in the elegant apartment and drink with Bradley, who wore a steel brace on his leg after falling from a horse, and with the two young Stenson sisters, who looked so much alike, and he would wonder, as he always did, which one Bradley slept with, or did he sleep with both? "Joe, tell Mr. Bradley I'm coming up," he said to the doorman.

The snow was now streaming over the entrance, and across the road the children were screeching, throwing snowballs at each other as the stout woman tried to round them up. She came herding them across the street and around the corner and into the light of the lounge entrance. "Have a happy Christmas," called the bag lady, who was at the curb, ready to cross the street, her eye on the lot and the shelter of that one old car, the way to it blocked by another car crawling up to the curb. For the second time this week, Rodney Smith the cabinet minister, one of those patrons who never entered the lounge, was there in his big black limousine. Alfred the driver, in his blue uniform and cap, got out and was heading for the entrance when Smith called suddenly from the back seat, "Wait a minute, Alfred." While Alfred stood in the snow, the big-shouldered handsome cabinet minister leaned back, looking out at the street and pondering. The street was a black shiny strip with little white margins at the curbs. Three months after the death of his wife, Rodney Smith had married a much younger woman whom he had met in a doctor's office. His friends had warned him that she was hard-eyed, but he had been excited by her youth and beauty. His work made it necessary that he keep an apartment in the city. She refused to leave his fine home in the Caledon Hill where she invited her own friends. Alfred would go into the lounge, pick out a girl from the block, bring her to the car, and drive to the apartment. Tonight the falling snow made Rodney Smith think of the old days at home on Christmas Eve and his son with him at the tree. And if his son had gone to Caledon tonight and was waiting, there would be warmth in his company: the warmth he needed. Sighing, he lowered the car window and called, "Alfred," beckoning, and said, "Caledon, Alfred. We're going to Caledon." Alfred got quickly into the car, avoiding two neighborhood patrons coming out of the lounge.

One was a little short fat guy and the other was heavy-set and bald. Both were wearing windbreakers. The little fat guy, holding out his palms and lifting his face, cried happily, "I didn't know it was snowing. When did it start to snow? I feel like a kid," and his friend said, "Yeah, it's great. It feels so mild. Remember when we used to go to midnight mass, walking in the snow. Let's go back to the lounge and have a few beers till midnight. Then we can walk over to the cathedral."

The lounge was a large panelled room, the panelling dark from age, the room dimly lit; the oak tables, there for years, were carefully polished and preserved, as were the comfortable leather-backed chairs. It was like a big clubroom. Those who remained from the old Anglo-Saxon neighborhood were at the corner tables nearest the entrance, still keeping to themselves, some drunk, some playing cards, some telling jokes, one joke after another, no conversation, just jokes. In the centre of the room there were tables for the new people and strangers.

At one table, two old men played checkers. At another, a long-haired, scholarly thin man with steel spectacles was reading to his friends from a German newspaper. The waiter made sure everyone kept drinking. In the corner to the left, and farthest from the entrance, there was a table with three empty chairs, as if the table were reserved, or as if patrons knew better than to try and take it over. This corner was a haven for thieves and petty criminals. Red Horgan, who had once worked for Edmund J. Dubuque, was there, as was Jonas Pyle, the daytime burglar who had never been convicted, and Frankie Spagnola, the pimp with the curling black hair and fine white teeth, a style-setter; he had taken to wearing three-piece dark suits and thought he looked like a banker. They all felt secure in the Bradley; the peace of the Bradley was upon them. On this snowy evening, with its welcoming lights the hotel looked like a magic sanctuary, which was what the lounge was. But if a stranger came in and stood looking around, many eyes turned on him and he felt there was something menacing in the sense of security they all seemed to share.

To the right, far from the thieves' corner, three tables were drawn together. This was "the block", where six girls, all under thirty, all on the same side of the tables, faced the patrons. Joyce, Marilyn, Stevie, the mulatto Irene, Daphne—the only tall one—Hildegarde, the thin German girl—and a place for Ellie, tall and beak-nosed, who was out with a John. They had the faces of girls from small towns or suburban high schools, faces still open and friendly but without any of the mysterious expectancy of youth. All jolly and joking, they were contented in their privileged places. On holidays, when not working on the block, they hung around together, and one Sunday last summer they had organized a picnic, going across the lake on a boat. They tried, too, to organize a softball team, but couldn't find another team that would play them.

At the back of the lounge and across the width of the big room was an eight-foot-high lattice grill. Behind the grill stood the long, splendid brass-and-mahogany bar with its great mirror, and behind the bar was Gil in his white shirt and black bow-tie, Gil with his smooth good looks, his blue candid eyes and knowing little smile. The lattice grill was his window on the lounge.

It was more than just another bar in Gil's life. In many bars in many cities he had seen a thousand faces and judged them, but this bar in his home town was the one he had wanted. At this hour there was only one vacant stool. On the other stools were regulars—Swanson the lawyer and a colleague, with their discontented young wives, who did not want to be at home on Christmas Eve; the two beautiful girls who read the news on the television stations accompanied now by the fat, bumptious actor with the Scottish accent; three regulars from the racing crowd; Jim Collins, the newspaper columnist just back from China; and, for the first time, two girls from Rosedale with their escorts. As these girls drank, they grew more exhilarated and more inclined to turn on their stools and peer through the lattice. Some of the regulars did this, too, unconsciously. It was as if, at particular moments, they all felt a malevolent chill coming through the grill from the lounge like a puff of air on their necks, quickening them and making them imagine they could hear a nearby whispered death sentence. In the centre of the lattice grill was a swinging door. Only a man with confidence or gall would dare come through that door.

Judge Gibbons approached the one vacant stool. "How are you, Gil? A Scotch. And take one for yourself." He leant closer. "Look," he whispered confidentially, "this hasn't been a good night for me. I can't talk to Bradley. Everything becomes a sardonic joke. Do you think you could find a little time?"

Then the lattice door from the lounge swung in, and those at the bar turned, startled, as a stocky man in an expensive brown cloth coat with an otter collar pushed his way in and took a step toward the bar. It was an off-balanced step, for he had a club foot and wore a heavy boot with a sole three inches thick. His name was Edmund J. Dubuque, but ever since boyhood he had been called Da Boot because of this heavy shoe, which he could use as a deadly weapon. A solid, broad-shouldered man, he had arms that looked like short legs attached to his shoulders. His hairline had receded, giving him a forehead that looked as noble as the Judge's. His hard brown eyes, never shifting, never changing, were the compelling eyes of a man who knew he no longer had to make noise to get attention. He had the proud and self-sufficient air of one who owned not only this place, but the whole neighborhood. He thought he did own it. If he didn't own it, who did? Not the local alderman, or the local landlords who paid rental tribute to him.

He had been born in the neighborhood in the same block as Gil. But his father, a shiftless crazy dreamer and a drunk, had discovered the Bible and the great commercial possibilities in preaching, and had fled from his wife, who then worked herself to death cleaning the floors of office buildings late at night. Dubuque had started off his business career as a bill collector for a furrier, then as an enforcer for a loan shark. Now everyone in the neighborhood knew him. Some little shops, owned by nervous immigrants who were aware he knew every burglar in the neighborhood, paid him for protection. He also loaned money and collected money for others. He did favors for neighbors. Fathers having trouble with their sons often came to his panelled office in the Olympic Trust Building. It was no wonder he had a proud authoritative air now as he took a step toward Gil. Smiling, standing behind the Judge, he said, "I just dropped in, Gil, to wish you the compliments of the season." Taking one look at him, the Judge muttered, "Some other time, Gil," gulped down his drink, and fled.

"What's the matter with him?" Dubuque asked.

"Maybe he thinks he'll see you in his court," Gil said, grinning.

"That'll be the day," Dubuque said disdainfully, taking the Judge's stool. "A man like that doesn't know anything. That's why he threw that girl in jail. I read about it, Gil. Contempt of court. All he knows about is the law. He doesn't know anything about justice. So, how're you doing?"

2

"IT'S BEEN A ROUGH DAY, ED," GIL SAID.

"Yeah, what's the trouble?"

"It's my brother. I've been to the hospital a couple of times today. A second heart attack."

"I remember Philip."

"Yeah, Philip."

"What does he do?"

"Industrial design."

"Must've made some money."

"He got along. I think he's dying."

"Wait a minute. Don't say that. They do wonders these days."

"No," Gil said, then faltered, shocked to find himself talking about his brother to Dubuque. He hadn't told anyone else in the hotel, and he had no friendship with Dubuque, who only came into the bar from time to time to amuse himself and to show that he had been a part of Gil's life. "Sure I remember him," Dubuque

11

went on. "I remember when we were kids he didn't like me. Looked down his nose at me. That's all right," he said, grinning. "I kicked him on the shin once. Nearly broke his leg. I didn't like him. Aw hell, what do kids know about each other? You were a family. I envied you. Now I've got my own very big family—the neighborhood," he said indulgently.

Not listening, his mind on the hospital, Gil put out his hands, as if he had never seen them before. Dubuque said, "Hey, Gil, I'm still here," but Gil was seeing himself in the hospital corridor on his way to Philip's room; he saw a woman in the waiting room at the end of the corridor, beckoning. "You're Gil," she said when he was close, and when he put out his hand she started to cry. She was a pretty woman of forty with dark hair and strange slanted eyes, half Oriental, her hair untidy, her face puffy from crying. He said to her gently, "You're Lenore." When they sat down she said, "I always understood why you didn't want to get involved. The family and all. Maybe it was better, but I know all about you, Gil."

Philip had a wife and two children, but the only real joy he had ever known with a woman he had found in Lenore. Hard-working and respectable, Philip had tried to keep Lenore hidden. His wife, Alice, had never been able to complain that she was humiliated publicly. Alice herself was a good straightforward girl, whom Philip had married when he was nineteen. She had refused to grow into Philip's life, and when he began to do well in his business and became fascinated by painters and painting, she had shown no interest. When he wanted to take her out to dinner or parties with his painter friends, she would tell him to go by himself; she visited her mother. She knew nothing about this woman

Lenore, her face wet with tears, who said, "I've been here for hours; his wife is in there with him, just sitting beside him. She won't let me see him, Gil."

"The poor woman," he said, "poor Philip, too." He had taken Lenore's hand, and when he let it go she reached out suddenly and took his hand, and, turning it slowly, straightening the fingers, she started to cry, "Oh, dear God, you have hands just like his, Gil," she said.

"You shouldn't stay here," he said. "I know," she said. He took her down to the street door and got her in a taxi. When he returned to the nurses' station they told him he could see Philip for just a minute. Alice had left. Philip whispered to him, "Lenore . . . here . . . what harm would it have done . . . ?"

While these things were in Gil's mind, Dubuque went on talking and remembering till Hazel, who helped at the bar, told Gil there was a phone call. As he moved down the bar, he looked so worried that faces turned, eyes following him. The voice on the phone said quietly, "This is the hospital. You left your number. We are very sorry. Everything that could be done was done . . ." and he said calmly, "Thank you. I'll come down and make the arrangements," yet he cried out within himself, "My brother is —," then couldn't say the word "dead" because it was like a tearing at his flesh. When his breathing became easier he said to Hazel, "I must go at once to my father's house. A death in the family. Look after everything." Then he got his overcoat from the office and crossed the street to his car on the lot.

It was now about eleven o'clock and still snowing, with about an inch on the ground, but it was so mild the snow would be gone by morning. The family home was only five minutes away by car, and as he drove down Parliament Street and turned along the side street leading to the big park where he and Philip had played with their sleighs and learned to skate, he kept repeating, "Some Christmas present for them, some Christmas present." It was a street of rundown houses beside others renovated into townhouses, and there were red Christmas lights in many windows, and lights around doors. His family's small house of red brick, halfway along the street, had always been well kept and freshly painted. As he neared it, his car lights picked up a figure walking slowly along the sidewalk in the snow, a small man with an erect posture, his right shoulder down a little as Philip's right shoulder had always been lowered, too. His father, carrying a small paper bag. Slowing down, Gil let him get as far as their house, then before he could turn in Gil got out of the car and called, "Dad." In his soft, even voice his father called, "Hello, Gil. I wondered when you'd be in. You always come on Christmas Eve." And holding up the paper bag he said, "Your mother is worried, you know, and she said, 'I'd like some ice cream.' You know how she likes ice cream, and I was glad to hear her say it. I knew the restaurant would be open. I got her a brick of ice cream."

"Dad," he began, taking his father's arm as they went up the walk to the door, "it's bad news about Philip," and his father, not asking for the news, stood still and there was a long silence with the veil of falling snow between them as Gil began, "He's . . ." but then he couldn't say "dead". In an even, quiet tone, he said, "Well, one of us is in another world now."

"Gil," his father said finally, "you tell your mother, will you?"

"I'll tell her." And they went into the house and through to the kitchen, where his mother was sitting in the armchair near the grate of an old-fashioned coal stove that had been in the kitchen as long as Gil could remember. Some red coals were glowing in the open grate, just as they had glowed when he was a kid and would come in with his mitts soaking and his mother would hang the wet mitts in front of the grate. Her hair now was white, her face lined, but she had kept a girl's expression in her very blue eyes. Whenever he had been far from home thinking of his mother, he had remembered her blue eyes. When she saw him there with his father, she stood up, frightened, her eyes shifting from his face to his father's, and she said, "Gilbert, did your father tell you about a strange phone call from Alice at dinnertime? She said a woman was trying to see Philip at the hospital. Isn't that awful? A woman crying. Do you know anything about this woman, Gilbert?"

"Sit down, Mother," Gil said gently and she did, yet couldn't take her eyes off his face. Now there are just the three of us, he thought, just the three of us now. "Look, Mother, try and take it easy, please," he said quietly. "Philip's gone. He didn't make it."

"Oh, oh, oh," she wailed, and her cry was desolate as she rose in the chair. He said sternly, "Don't, don't, Mother, don't go on, it's bad enough for us. Crying will make it worse. You mustn't cry, do you hear? If you cry it'll be terrible. Now don't." Afraid of her tears, he sounded angry. "Sit down." Shaken, she nodded obediently. "I'm not crying. I understand, Gilbert. I won't make it worse. I won't, Gilbert," and when he sat down the three of them were silent, each afraid of the others' silence.

All the years of their lives were in this silence in that kitchen. His father's grey eyes hadn't changed their expression. His father had got what he wanted in his life: to own his own home, owe no money, have his family, and say what he wanted to say. He was a very articulate man and all he said now, breaking the silence, was, "Peg . . ."

"What, Joe?"

"Do you remember Philip's little yellow suit?"

"Yellow velvet. When he was four. I remember, Joe." Her eyes began to fill with tears, and then, remembering she had been told not to cry, she swallowed and sat back stiffly on the chair.

"Mother, Mother," Gil said, feeling stricken as he went to her and kissed her hand, "cry if you want to. Why shouldn't you cry now? It's a good thing, Mother," and he was ashamed that in protecting himself from the panic within him he had denied his mother her tears, ashamed, he knew, because it was something he might remember the rest of his life. "It's all right, Gilbert," she said. "When I'm alone, I'll cry," and he let her be.

"Gil, tell us something," his father said.

"What is it?"

"Alice talked to us late this afternoon. It must have been very hard on her to find another woman thinking she had a right to be with Philip when his life was ending. Alice was outraged."

"Did you know about this, Gilbert?" his mother asked.

"Yes, I knew about it. I kept away from it."

"Do you know this woman?"

"I hardly met her."

"Not Philip! It's not like Philip," his father protested. "I was so close to Philip. He was so straight. To hear this now . . . Gil, Philip had a wife and children."

"Now listen to me," he blurted out, startling them. "Philip looked after his wife and children. He never hurt Alice. He loved his children. Yes, Alice was a good woman, but she never wanted to share Philip's life or share his dreams. Good as she was, she could never make Philip feel she found joy and wonder in being with him. No ecstasy. She couldn't be his companion. Then he found this woman, this Lenore, and he found love and sacrifice in her, and yes, wonder in being together. Without it, it's a dead life for a man. He found life in Lenore. Yet it was a secret thing, they kept it a hidden thing so you two and Alice would not be hurt, and all that Lenore asked was to see him before he died. Oh, Mother, don't you see?"

In the silence, his father sat with his arms folded, his grey eyes unchanging, his mother, her head on the side, trying to see her dead son as she had never seen him before. "All in secret, a secret," she whispered, half dreaming.

"That was Philip," he said.

"I thought I knew my own son," his father said. "Didn't I know him at all? Peg . . . Peg . . ." he said, turning to her, for she was lost in her own thoughts.

"It's like a story," she said suddenly. "Yes, a story," and as she repeated it, the wonder in her eyes and in her changing face startled Gil. The hurt, lost look had gone. The light of her wonder and dreams was all in her brightening blue eyes, as if her dead son was now taking on a new life in her imagination.

"You're right," Gil said. "It's quite a story," and feeling better about her, he said he must go to the hospital to make all the arrangements. They asked him to have a cup of tea with them. His mother ate the ice cream. They talked about Philip's children and what could be done for them.

When Gil left them he stood for a moment on the sidewalk, looking back at the house, and knew why he had talked to Dubuque and not to others who were closer to him. Dubuque had hit Philip as a boy. Philip had said that Dubuque wanted to grow up to be the biggest criminal in town. Everything Philip said about Dubuque had turned out right. And yet the relationship had been about living, a personal, even bitter thing. To Hazel at the bar, or to Mr. Bradley, he could only say, "My brother is dead." But to Dubuque, "Philip is dead."

Then, driving carefully on the slippery street, he thought of his mother's changing face and the light coming into her eyes when she whispered, "It's like a story," as if she knew she could keep Philip alive in a story. It was the truth. He must have known this himself some years ago, Gil thought, known it when he left college and began his wandering, believing he would become a writer. And what a beginning he'd had; just two years after graduate school he'd had a poem and a story printed in the *Paris Review*. But after that, nothing! Without noticing, he drove through a red light, but no cop was on the corner and it was snowing harder.

3

DUBUQUE, TOO, WAS IN HIS CAR, ON HIS WAY TO settle a problem with a woman who was giving him some trouble. This was a new experience; women rarely gave him trouble. He spoke their language. It was not a gift; it was knowledge from long experience. He had come to believe that a woman was either born to be a saint and didn't know it, or a whore and didn't know it, but it was up to him to know, and he thought he did know because all his boyhood training had told him about such things.

His awareness of the peculiar nature of women began when he was a kid, watching his mother. The neighbors used to say she was a blunt, harsh, bitter woman, abandoned by her crazy hypocritical husband and growing old and beaten before her time, scrubbing floors at night in office buildings. But Dubuque thought he had seen, or maybe he wanted to believe, that her blunt harshness was just a protective mask; she was a suffering saint. He loved her till the day she died. But at night, when she worked, he had been left alone in the house. Down the street was a woman he called "the Cookie Lady" and she took him into her house and let him sleep there and gave him milk and cookies. In the house, the prostitutes who worked for her made a pet of him, and while he ate his milk and cookies or read comic books, they would forget he was there and gossip and talk about their bodies and joke about men and burlesque their antics, and he acquired all their wisdom as well as some of his own, watching and listening to the Cookie Lady talk about the girls.

Even now when he was a boss man in his neighborhood, and had to threaten a client for being short on payment of a loan, he would explain things first to the client's wife. His connection with the wives came about through his contacts with bookies in the neighborhood. The wife of one of his shopkeeper debtors told him her husband owed all his money to a bookie. Dubuque had the bookie spread the word around that the husband was cut off; no more bets. His wife passed the word to other suffering wives and so Dubuque became a presence in their homes. It reached the point that a wife having money problems with her husband would sometimes come to his office to consult him. Indeed, Joe Hiltz, a bookie who had a big tobacco store and newsstand, and who paid Dubuque protection money, had come to him about a problem with his wife. Later Joe had said in the Bradley lounge, "Don't ask me about women. Edmund J. Dubuque is the only man I know who understands women."

The girl whom he was bent on seeing at this hour on Christmas Eve, a twenty-four-year-old primary school teacher, was one of those clients he had started to gather around him in the days when he was a collector of bad debts for a furrier. One cold February morning he had gone to see a young broker's wife on the hill who owed two hundred and fifty dollars on a fur coat. He was to get the two hundred and fifty or take the coat. The half-asleep young woman who came to the door in an open thin blue negligee, her mouth a smear of lipstick, smiled at him drowsily, and he nodded and took his time. While they were having a cup of tea he told her he knew an out-of-town businessman who would pay three hundred to have dinner with her. When he was leaving, he left his card. At this time there was a furriers' convention at the Royal York. He knew some of the furriers quite well. He heard from the broker's wife.

From then on it was easy—the business developed, mainly by word of mouth, and now it was taking up too much of his time. This schoolteacher, whose first encounter he had arranged, now had her own arrangement with the client. She had been set up in an apartment on a street of renovated houses turned into expensive places with big windows giving a view from the hill of the downtown city. When he knocked, Miss Grant, a very fresh-faced, clean-looking, short-haired blonde wearing horn-rimmed glasses, came to the door. She had been wrapping Christmas presents, and they were in a little pile on a table. "Oh Dubuque, it's you," she said, blocking the way. A tall girl in a pink turtleneck sweater, she drew back at a loss for words as he brushed by her, looking around. The big remodelled room had a large picture window. Sauntering over, he stood looking down at the lighted core of the city in the snow, the rash of lights running west and east, all gleaming in the snow: his city!

"Nice place you've got here, Miss Grant," he said.

"I like it, yes."

"You're a naughty girl, you know."

"What do you want, Mr. Dubuque? I'm busy."

"Yes, you're naughty. You see, I think you should know that whatever your arrangement with Mr. Alford is, it should have been made through me."

"You're out of my life, Mr. Dubuque."

"Not while you're with Mr. Alford. I want my cut, Miss Grant."

"Get out of here."

"I don't like greedy women, Miss Grant."

"And I don't like pimps. Coming here after money. Like any other goddamned pimp."

Seizing her by the shoulders, he threw her over the back of the chesterfield, then grabbed a thick Christmas-wrapped book, and pounded her bottom with it while she hung over the chesterfield. He pounded and pounded till she cried out, then he let her crawl to the floor. Kneeling there, frightened, she waited. "As for me and what I am, Miss Grant, I don't go after any woman," he said calmly. "They come to me, seeking favors, like you did. I don't think I even shook hands with you, let alone pat your fanny, or ask you to show me the goods, or make me your one sweet lover. I only do good things for women. Well, you're off my list. So peddle your fanny some place else, little schoolteacher." With a disdainful shrug, he walked out and got into his black Cadillac and drove back down the hill on his way home. He cut to the left, going through Rosedale, heading for his own neighborhood. Snow streaming across his car lights had melted on the road, making it a gleaming black strip under his headlights. No one was out walking. People in this neighborhood used their cars. The streets were tree-lined, and leaves that had fallen from the trees lay uncollected in great piles by the roadside, looking like mounds of snow. He came to the street that ran alongside the southern ravine. The big old houses with their lighted windows and high fences made the road seem dark—everything in heavy shadows. Then he saw headlights coming toward him, and at the big stone corner house, as the oncoming car slowed down, the door swung open. Then there was a wild scream as a woman jumped or was pushed out, there, right under Dubuque's headlights on the shining black pavement, and the other car, its door pulled closed, speeded up and shot away. Stopping his Cadillac, he limped over to the woman, who lay stiff and still, curled up under a long fur coat. "Miss? Hey, miss," he said.

He didn't know whether she was hurt or stunned and couldn't hear him, for dogs had started to bark. All these big houses had dogs: Great Danes, boxers, Irish wolfhounds, black Labradors; even the poodles were giant poodles. The dog in the stone house had started barking loudly and the bark, taken up by the dog next door, was answered in every house along the street. Lights came on. "Hey, miss," Dubuque repeated, bending over her. When he touched her shoulder, she rolled to her knees, crouching, staring at the wet pavement, her long hair falling over her face. "Are you all right, miss?" Then, her hand came out groping, as if she could not see him but was reaching for his voice. Helping her to her feet, holding her in his arms when she swayed, he half dragged her over to the curb and let her sit down. Her head fell into her hands. "Are you all right, miss? What happened?" he asked.

Her voice broke as she went to speak; then, raising her head, trying to look around, she said jerkily, "He came at me and I jumped. My knee," she said. But her hand was now on the back of her head.

A young black-haired woman in a squirrel coat came from the doorway of the big stone house. "Is she all right?" this young woman asked. "I heard the scream and looked out the window and saw her on the road. I phoned the police. I live here. I'm Mrs. Loney."

"She's hurt her knee," Dubuque said. As Mrs. Loney sat down beside the girl, Dubuque saw the purse on the wet road, and he picked it up, along with the contents that had rolled into the gutter: a lipstick, a compact, some keys. Standing in the headlights of his car, packing the things back in the purse, he looked for some identification. There was only a ten-dollar bill folded in a side pocket. Coming back to the curb, he put the purse in the girl's lap. From this angle, with the high street light falling on her, he saw that her long coat was mink. He knew furs; he had picked up many a mink coat in his days as a bill collector. "What does she say?" he asked Mrs. Loney.

"Very little. She's confused. She says she's all right."

"Her head," Dubuque said, taking his glove off and touching the girl's head. The hair was very fine. His fingers kept going lightly against her scalp, then to the back of her head, and to the spot on her head where he had seen her put her hand. A bump was there. His fingers felt damp. He held his fingers up to the light. There was a little blood on them.

"A doctor should look at that bump," he said.

"No," the girl mumbled, her head on her knees.

"Any kind of a head injury should get hospital attention," said Mrs. Loney, her groomed head silvered by the falling snow, her face full of sympathy as she put her arm very gently around the girl.

"No, I'll go home," the girl said dully.

"Where do you live, miss?" Dubuque asked. "Far from here?"

"Across the viaduct," she said. She had a little accent, a very faint accent.

"What's your name?"

"Ilona. Ilona Tomory."

"Look, Ilona," Dubuque said, "I can take you home. It's no trouble." Looking up, she saw his expensive black coat with the fur collar, and then his black Cadillac just twenty feet away. As she did so, he saw her face for the first time: the high cheekbones, hollowing cheeks, or maybe the shadows did this . . . a face fit for that long mink coat, and in the car lights her shoulder-length brown hair had flecks of gold in it; in that snowy light her eyes were scared and staring.

Mrs. Loney said gently, "Ilona, listen, Ilona. If you'd rather, I could get my own car. It's right there in the garage," and she pointed to her driveway. "And I could take you home."

"You could both come in my car," Dubuque said. "How about it, Ilona?"

"If she'd come too."

"Of course I'll come," Mrs. Loney said.

"Can you stand up?" Dubuque asked. But while he had his hand under the girl's arm, Mrs. Loney said, "There's the police car." The yellow police car with its red flashers was at the end of the street, and when it turned the wrong way, Mrs. Loney ran out to the middle of the road, waving her arms.

"Never mind the police. Tell them it's all right," Ilona pleaded, but by this time the police car had come backing along the street. The two officers who got out seemed too young and fresh-faced. "This girl was thrown out of a car," Dubuque said. Mrs. Loney said, "I heard the scream. I called you. I'm Mrs. Loney." One of the officers, the taller one, his face unmarked and untroubled by his police life, bent down beside Ilona. "Was the man sexually assaulting you?" he asked bluntly.

"Yes," she whispered.

"Did he try to rape you?"

"Yes."

"Do you want to lay a charge?"

"No. No."

"You should lay a charge."

"I want to get home. Let me go home."

"If she won't lay a charge, there's nothing we can do, unless she'd like us to take her home," he said to Dubuque. "That's the trouble with these cases. The girls get nervous about going into court."

"Let them take me home," Ilona said. But when she tried to stand up by herself, Dubuque and Mrs. Loney had to support her.

"That's your car, eh sir?" the officer said, looking with approval at the Cadillac, then at Dubuque's coat, and then at the great big stone house in which Mrs. Loney lived.

While they walked the girl slowly across the road, with one officer accompanying them, the other went back to the police car to talk to the station. "We can all sit in the front seat," Dubuque said, half lifting the girl into his car, then gallantly assisting Mrs. Loney, too.

The officer talking on the radio got out of his car, beckoning to his colleague. After conferring, they walked out to the middle of the road, swinging their flashlights back and forth and around on the pavement, then along the snow-filled curbs, moving over to the snow by the fence, and then they poked around under low bushes close to Mrs. Loney's fence. Finally, they came back.

"You'll have to get out of the car, miss," one said.

"You'll have to get into our car," the other said.

"Now just a minute," said Dubuque, out of the car and coming across the headlights to the officers. "The girl's in bad shape. Leave her alone. Don't ask her to hop from one car to another. What's the matter, anyway?"

"Sorry," the officer with the big shoulders said. "She has to come with us. They say at the station a charge has been laid against her."

"A charge? What's the charge?"

"Robbery."

"What is this?" Dubuque protested. "I saw her thrown out of the car."

"Yeah, but the man drove right down to the station," the cop said. "Says he was trying to take her to the station. She had his wallet. She jumped out with his wallet. Five hundred dollars in the wallet." Leaning into the car, he said firmly, "You'll have to get into our car, miss."

Without a word, the girl got out and, with surprising strength and control, limped to the police car. "We'll get this thing straightened out at the station," the big-shouldered cop said to Dubuque. "If you think you saw what happened, sir, come to the station."

"You bet I will, I'll follow right along. It'll be all right, Mrs. Loney," he said, turning to her.

"The poor girl, the poor thing. What are they trying to do to her? I'm glad you're going along, Mr. . . . ."

"Dubuque. Edmund J. Dubuque."

"I'm glad they took my name, Mr. Dubuque," and after Dubuque started his car, following the police along the street, he looked back. Mrs. Loney, crestfallen, remained in the middle of the road.

It was only a five-minute drive to the station, which was in Dubuque's neighborhood and the newest thing on the block: a bright, clean-looking yellow brick building with glass-block windows. Right behind the officers and the girl, Dubuque walked into the station. There was a sergeant with a bald head and heavy black moustache at the desk. The girl, still in some pain, or maybe dazed, stood at the desk, hardly aware the officers were talking to the sergeant. Then, without questioning her, the desk sergeant beckoned to a man who had been sitting by himself on a shiny oaken wall-bench. The man's overcoat, folded neatly, was on the arm of the bench. When he stood up in his well-pressed dark-grey suit, he looked like a severe, conservative bookkeeper or accountant. In a crowd, he might have looked like a lonely man who had never had much fun, but now his pale-blue eyes were full of nervous energy.

"Yeah, that's the one," he said.

"Your name, miss?"

"Ilona Tomory."

"Ilona . . . speak up. Ilona what?"

"Tomory."

"This man, Mr. Smiley, says you were at the Bradley Hotel. Is it true?" The question startled Dubuque.

"I was there," she whispered.

"Now you tell me what happened, sir," the sergeant said, turning to Smiley.

"I took her out to my car," Smiley said coolly. "We were to go to another hotel she uses. Suddenly she said she wanted to drive around a bit, and did I have the money? So we drove around. I showed her the money, then she had her arms around me, loving me up, but then

I felt her hand in my breast pocket. Out of the corner of my eye I saw her slipping my wallet into her purse and there was five hundred dollars in the wallet. I grabbed at her, she yelled, and she jumped out. . . ."

"You didn't stop. Why didn't you go after her and your wallet?"

"I headed right here for this station. I knew you'd get her."

"It's not true," she said, her voice shaking. Ashamed, scared, or dazed, she managed to be dignified. "As soon as I got into the car I didn't like him. I don't like him. I wanted to get out. He wouldn't let me get out."

"Oh, Christ," Smiley said scornfully.

"Where's the money, lady?" the sergeant asked.

"I never saw his wallet," she said quietly. "I never saw any money."

"You picked him up."

"He picked me up." Then came her silence, utter silence, and this silence, a kind of stillness, was so impressive the sergeant himself didn't seem sure how he should treat her.

"All right," he said gruffly, "let's see your purse."

As she handed over the purse, Dubuque stepped forward with all his indulgent authority. "I was a witness to some of this," he said. "The name is Dubuque," he added importantly. Opening his coat, he took out his wallet, from which he took a card, "Edmund J. Dubuque—The Olympic Trust Building."

"Dubuque," said the sergeant. "Oh, Mr. Dubuque," he added respectfully, "I thought I recognized you." But Dubuque had come to believe that all policemen respected him.

"You should know Dubuque," the sergeant said to

the cops. "How come you don't know him?" and he grinned at the arresting officers. They explained that Mr. Dubuque had been in the company of Mrs. Loney, who lived in the big corner house. With Mrs. Loney, Dubuque did not seem to be Dubuque.

"Grow up, officer," Dubuque said calmly. "Well, this is what I saw. There was a scream and this girl was pushed out of the car as it almost came to a stop, and she fell and there she was lying on the road under my headlights. I helped her. Then a woman came out of her house and joined us. I saw the purse on the road. Stuff had fallen out of the purse. I picked it up. It was all there under my headlights. No wallet. Absolutely. No roll of money either, officer. I can tell you everything that was in the purse. Item by item. I picked all the stuff up."

"She could have thrown the wallet away."

"Falling out of the car, no sir! Thrown it where? We all looked."

"It's snowing. It's in the snow somewhere. My money's somewhere and she's got it." Smiley said, working himself up. "You bitch!" he said, turning on Ilona. "Where is it?"

"We looked all around the scene. Of course, it *is* snowing," the tall cop said.

"Maybe I picked it up," Dubuque said, grinning.

"I didn't say you did," Smiley said. "Sergeant, what is this? Why don't you search her?"

"All right. The coat, Bradford," the sergeant said to the tall cop. Sticking his hands in the coat pocket, Bradford found only gloves and a handkerchief. "Okay," the sergeant said. "Mr. Smiley, do you think she's got the wallet hidden on her person?"

"Yes, why don't you have me searched?" she asked

with a faint smile as she recovered her self-possession.

"Well, now, how are we going to straighten this out?" the sergeant asked. "Are you laying a charge, Mr. Smiley?"

"How can I lay a charge?" Smiley said angrily. "No one's backing me up. No one's with me."

"And you, lady, what about you? Are you laying a charge of attempted rape?"

"No," she whispered, her head down again. "How could I go through with it? . . . My mother and father . . ."

"Well, then . . ."

"Could I go home now?"

"There's no charge being laid. Go ahead. . . ."

"Hey, what about my money?" Smiley asked.

"What money?" Dubuque asked innocently. "There wasn't any money."

"Is there a phone here?" she asked. "Can I use it?" She had taken a comb from her purse and was combing her hair.

"There you are," the sergeant said, pointing along the desk to the telephone.

"Thanks for your help, Mr. Dubuque," she said, turning to him like a great lady. "You were very kind. Thank you."

While she was telephoning, Dubuque watched Mr. Smiley putting on the overcoat that he had left on the wall-bench. Still flushed with anger, Smiley did not look displeased at the outcome of his visit to the police station. Sauntering over to him, Dubuque said in an admiring tone, "You're a pretty smart customer, Mr. Smiley," and he tapped his head with his forefinger. "Quick up here, eh? That girl could have been killed, run over, or taken to the hospital. Well, you got here first. Nice going. You beat her to it, eh?"

"You go to hell," Smiley said, but something else, sticking in his mind and outraging him, made him blurt out viciously, "A goddamned cheap whore. Don't you understand? She's just a cheap whore."

"A whore?" Dubuque said, looking at her as she stood at the counter, her eyes on the open telephone book. "Well, obviously that's what you thought. You should get to know whores or you'll go on making mistakes. I read somewhere the whole world would squirm with lust if we didn't have whores. What about that?"

"What are you? Some goddamned pimp?"

"Hey," Dubuque said, dropping his eyes. "Your fly is still open."

"What? If you insult me . . ."

"Call a cop," Dubuque said, and when Smiley hurried out, he sauntered after him and watched him drive away.

As he stood by his own Cadillac, waiting for Ilona Tomory to come out, his wonder about her quickened: she was in the doorway's harsh light, aloof and pale and out of place in her long mink coat, under the lighted police station sign. The snow was coming down hard and he called, "Can I give you a lift?"

"No, thank you," she said quickly. "I've got a taxi," and while she waited, he couldn't turn away. When the taxi arrived, she was out in the heavily falling snow. In the strong bright light from the station-house entrance, the snow swirled around her, the flakes in the light dancing around her head. In no time, the snow whitened the long mink coat. Then, moving towards the taxi, she was a tall and superior white lady coming out of the brightness into the shadows. Something about her suddenly jarred Dubuque's vast sense of certainty about things, and as she got into the taxi he called out, "Lady . . ."

"What?"

"Who are you?" But the taxi was moving away.

4

IT TURNED MUCH COLDER. WINTER HAD SETTLED IN. It was the week when the Dubuque house was readied for his neighborhood festive-season party. His sand-blasted remodelled house with wrought-iron railings on the steps was just a block away from the ramshackle house where he had been born. It had no garage. He rented a garage at the end of a fifty-foot lane, five doors away from his house. His close neighbors were new people—"white-painters", they were called—an academic and a young advertising man, and their busy independent wives. But Dubuque did not like his own wife to be too friendly with these women. His house, except for the neighborhood party he gave every year, was a secluded place where he never did business. His wife, a small, dark, sweet-faced woman with a voluptuous figure, was a home-loving girl, as her grandmother and mother had been before her, and shrewd as she was, she never asked questions about his business. He had met her when he had been in the hospital with pneumonia. As his nurse, she had been fascinated by his hard defiance of sickness, and his fierce sense of himself in the face of death. One of the few things his father had told him was, "Listen, little man, never marry a beautiful woman, you hear? Remember this when you grow up. If she's a beauty, other men will always be after her, and it'll always be worrying you. Marry a girl who'll be grateful as long as she lives."

His wife, he thought, was one of those women who had the saint in her and didn't know it. When he entered the house at night, he always waited to hear her call from the bedroom, "I'm here, Jay," and then, "Are you all right, Jay?" as if she had been fearing that someone had tried to kill him. Though she liked the big party, the one big party they had at the end of the year, she was bewildered by the wild and motley crew who came streaming into her orderly house to drink champagne, whiskey, vodka, brandy, gin, all on the table with a smiling bartender, and to eat the smoked salmon and chocolate Grand Marnier torte. All Dubuque's hench-men came to this party: his collectors, his muscle-men from the mortgage company he worked with, burglars, immigrant storekeepers who paid him for protection against break-ins, the local aldermen, some bookies, and two well-known sports writers who had drinks with Dubuque whenever he went to the fights. One of these sports writers, laughing as he explained that Peking duck was his favorite food, glanced around and said, "Looks like a jailbreak, doesn't it?" But after this big opulent party, the Dubuque house became a very private place again.

Two nights after the party, Dubuque was at the Bradley, but not in the lounge. He had come to the sedate side door, the entrance to Mr. Gilhooley's. He was wearing his coat with the fur collar and his expensive Russian fur hat. The doorman, recognizing, bowed in deference to the hat. In the bar, no one paid any attention to him; he was not one of the crowd, but when he found a stool and Gil came to him, he said, "I was going to write you a letter, Gil, but I thought I'd speak to you myself. I'm sorry about your brother, and for old times' sake I would like to have been at the funeral, but I had a hunch your father and mother would wonder why I was there. The same with flowers. It's why I didn't send flowers, though I wanted to."

"Forget it, Ed."

"It's Jay, now, like I said, Edmund Jay."

"Jay it is then, Ed."

"No, Jay it is then, Jay. Right?" Then, there seemed to be nothing to say, and after a moment of looking through the lattice at people in the lounge, Dubuque said, "Hear what happened to Big Mary?"

"No, I didn't."

"Cracked her head. Quite a fall to crack her head, eh?"

"Her heart?"

"No, her weight. Far too heavy," and it was then, still looking through the lattice, that Dubuque saw her. "That lady . . . why there she is. My God!"

"The lady?"

"In the coat there. The other night in the snow," and he quickly told Gil about the girl and the car and the police station. While he talked he kept his eyes on the girl, who seemed to be coming toward him with her long stride. Then, stunned, he faltered. With a faint smile she was approaching "the block"; then, sweeping by the girls there in her long mink coat, with the ease of a great lady, she took a table apart from the others. "What the hell is this, Gil?" Dubuque asked. "What's she doing there?"

"She works there."

"You've seen her before? You know her?"

"Just to say hello. For the last few weeks."

"But I've been in here on and off. I haven't seen her."

"She only comes in three times a week, I think."

"And I'm not coming in as much. Yeah, that's it." He suddenly felt uncertain about things. "Who is she, Gil?" he blurted out.

"A Hungarian."

"A Hungarian? Here like this?" and the bafflement in his face made Gil start to laugh.

"Well, don't let it upset you," Gil said.

"I'm not," Dubuque said. "But it's like that guy in the police station said. Don't you see, Gil. I didn't believe him. I can't believe this now."

"I thought you could always tell," Gil said.

"So I can. Don't worry. But I can also tell when something's wrong with the picture. I keep seeing her in that goddamn snowstorm. You seem to know her. What is she?"

"She came here and sat about where you're sitting a few months ago. . . . I remember her. I remember because she was with a young Hungarian, good-looking. He couldn't speak any English. They laughed a lot. She seemed to be showing him around. I talked to her about Hungary. She was born there but came here with her parents in '56, the Hungarian revolt, Cardinal Mind-szenty and all that stuff. Remember? It looked for a while like all Budapest was going to land in town, the sympathy for them got a bit ridiculous. I'm told there actually was a campaign to move the whole Budapest Opera Company here. A cultural blessing and all—and then someone pointed out that the local opera company wouldn't take too kindly to this. Now all those Hungarians you meet around here," Gil said smiling, "are, or were, aristocrats. Ever meet one who wasn't an aristocrat?"

"Yeah, an electrician. He overcharged me," and Dubuque turned to look through the lattice again, watching the girl intently, trying painfully to adjust his view of her, and he said, "How about the other broads? Don't they resent her, off by herself like that?"

"They call her the princess. First, they thought she gave them a little class, but she can't talk their language. You know the way it is with women nowadays," Gil said. "They all talk like truck-drivers. But I hear the Hungarian can't bring herself to tell Kitty Cat she's full of shit. Excuse me."

Shifting his head so he could see through the lattice, Dubuque watched a big fellow with thick, shining fair hair, and the ease of a man who knew exactly what he wanted, approach Ilona Tomory, order drinks, then begin his hard-eyed negotiation. Something went wrong. The big fellow slumped back in his chair, his confident grin turning into a scowl; then, suddenly gulping down his drink, he made some vicious remark and left her. "If she's a whore," Dubuque said, believing Gil was near him, "she can't do things like that. She'll get her teeth kicked in. What in hell is she up to?" Yet he could see that, sitting apart in that beautiful long fur coat draped around her shoulders, she was a magnetic promise of something the other girls couldn't offer. Just as Gil came back along the bar, bringing Dubuque a drink, another guy with a splashy blue tie, a very practical man, and by his manner an old hand, joined Ilona. He had a drink and a talk, and then, looking outraged, he shrugged and turned to Kitty Cat at her table. And Gil said, "You can't take your eyes off her?"

"No, I can't," Dubuque said. "I still don't know what in hell she's up to."

Then a middle-aged inconspicuous man with a receding hairline, and an overcoat on his arm, approached Ilona hesitantly, as if he knew that under her appraising eyes he must look like a lonely nobody. Sitting down, he beckoned the waiter. Plainly, he was a man who seemed to feel like a loser even when approaching a whore. Yet, she talked to him. She listened. They must be negotiating, Dubuque thought, assuming he knew exactly how it would go in whore's language. "How do you like it? Jig-a-jig, half and half? All around the world?"

"Who's the guy?" Dubuque asked. "What's he to her?"

"Search me," Gil said.

"A good friend, a Hungarian maybe?"

"Never saw him around here."

"My God, look at her," Dubuque said.

She had eyed the man carefully; then something he said, or something she saw in him, aroused her interest, and as she leaned closer, her lips parting, her face changed. It brightened, now full of curiosity. Her hand went out to his in gentle compassionate recognition that she was now dealing with no ordinary man. Surprised, or shaken by the warmth of the new life in her face, he looked around the room at the men at other tables. He really believed that she saw he was an interesting man; his face lit up.

She stood, and the man, never taking his eyes off

her as she smiled at him, walked with her to the door. "Well, I'll be damned," Dubuque said, and started to laugh. "I don't believe it. I've got to see it again."

"Stick around and you will," Gil said. "Give her an hour."

"The old 'angel of mercy' routine," Dubuque said. "No, it's more interesting. Look at the little guy. He feels like a somebody now. A little nobody suddenly sees he's a somebody! What's she got?"

"Something all her own, I guess," Gil said. "I don't know." Then, moving along the bar, he remembered how he had talked to his mother and father about his brother Philip's marriage—a bed without the new joys and new wonders Philip found with Lenore, and now it was as if Ilona had just given him a warming glimpse of his dead brother and Lenore.

Sipping his brandy and brooding, Dubuque looked up when Gil came his way again and said, "I'm still asking myself, a whore can't be personal?"

"That's right."

"It's as cold as a mackerel, eh?"

"Or she goes crazy. Yeah."

"I still ask what is she, Gil?"

"I don't think I'll ask," Gil said, smiling. "There's as much mystery in dirt and dung as there is in heaven."

"What?" Dubuque said. "Who says so?"

"It's what they say at the top of the mountain," Gil said, smiling.

"You've been on some mountain?"

"On my good nights."

"What's it like?"

"Things come in flashes, Jay."

"Don't kid me. Mountain tops are all snow, nothing but snow," but as he laughed, he had an illumination.

Maybe he could see why Ilona Tomory turned down the hard customers. Hard, confident guys threw her out of cars. It might be that with the lame, the halt, and the blind she felt safe. "Then again," he said to Gil, "maybe she's a crazy."

"Wired for sound!"

"Crazies are always onto their own things."

"Crazy, eh?" Gil said, serious now. "Well, let me tell you something. Remember the help I had before Hazel came on the job? Smitty. A great little guy, frayed nerves. The little guy liked Ilona from the first time she came around, and found ways of talking to her. But Smitty ended up going to hospital with a nervous break-down. Two weeks in the hospital and the doctors wanted him to try going home; he wouldn't. Imagine! Scared to go home; a place called home just another frightening place. He stayed in the hospital. Ilona heard about this and all on her own, without telling anybody, she marched down to the hospital and told Smitty to get dressed, she was taking him to the races, the trotters, and she took him out to the track and gave him money to bet on every race and got him laughing, then took him home. Smitty'll be all right, he'll be back. Maybe it takes a princess or a crazy to do something like that, Dubuque . . . excuse me." Some of his uptown admirers had come to the bar, and he had to leave.

But Dubuque could not leave; he waited, he watched for Ilona to return, and when she did, he watched her reject three men. A square-jawed, balding big fellow tried arguing, turned mean, and, standing up, raised his glass, ready to toss his drink down her dress. Then, thinking better of it, he called out some vicious insult. Laughing, Ilona made a lewd remark that made the girls on the block laugh, too. Then a little man, a half-apologetic, nondescript thirty-year-old man, who must have saved up his money for this, came clumsy and fumbling, waiting while she looked into his face. She touched his hand, talking to him, with curiosity and sympathy in her changing face. Here it comes now, now! Dubuque thought, and there it was—the gentle benediction, and in the little guy's eyes, the relief, the pride, the surprise. Smiling, she stood, her hand out, waiting for him to rise, then she, taller than he, led the way, passing those she had humiliated earlier, and one loud, brutal voice said, "Countess Cunt."

She stopped and, taking black gloves from a coat pocket, drew them on slowly, and then took the arm of the man with such an air of great dignity that he put back his head as they left the lounge. Dubuque, his heavy shoulders hunched, his eyes hard, was angry. In his life, everything had a price. He knew what was valuable. Here, he recognized that something of great price was being thrown away, before his eyes. "I don't understand this woman," he muttered. "I don't, I don't," and he didn't know that he scowled, and that the ugly scowl was attracting Gil's attention. "You know what it's like these days, Gil," he said anyway. "Just say how you want it. Well, she'll get her face smashed in. She's on her own. She'll get killed and it's too goddamn bad. I know guys on Bay Street who'd pay a big buck to have her in the right setting making them feel like that little guy feels now. Give me another brandy, Gil," and while drinking and thinking of rich, lonely businessmen, he found himself wondering what she was like under that splendid coat. Supposing she was flat-chested? It could be she knew she had to rely on the coat and on her acting skill to cast a spell on a guy, a spell she could make last the half-hour, and the guy wouldn't notice she had no breasts. Still scowling, he confused himself with these thoughts, for it hurt his pride to think she was a woman he didn't understand at all, and he asked for another brandy, then another, surprising Gil. It wasn't like Dubuque.

Leaving the bar, Dubuque stepped outside near the lounge entrance under the neon light hoping to see Ilona coming back along the street. It was bitterly cold. There was a heavy west wind, too, and, shivering, he turned up the collar of his coat. Bare strips on the road, usually black, were a dirty white and unmarked by passing cars. The ice along the curb was a dirty grey. A woman hurrying by had her head down, a scarf wrapped around her face. Limping away from the sheltered entrance, heading for his car parked on the lot, Dubuque kept repeating to himself, I don't understand the woman. Why couldn't she see that she could be a fabulous whore, a natural with a strange gift for creating the great illusion that makes a man feel that no matter what he has done, if she touched him he would feel excused and comforted, and interesting, too. To a lot of big important men she would be worth a bundle. Why couldn't she see it?

But there was another question, and it was worrying him in spite of all his proven wisdom about women: he wanted to know why a big-bucks hooker was giving her stuff away for peanuts to shabby little losers in ill-fitting suits, and in a place like the lounge. Why was she there at all? The question gnawed at him all the way home.

5

BUT THEN, FOR A WEEK, HE HAD TO DEAL WITH A threat to himself and his own business. It was the week of the cold wave. Two gentlemen from Miami, Victor Corelli and Marvin Feldstein, who were really from Montreal and henchmen for Big Joe Corona, came to town, got in touch with him, and suggested a sit-down in the Bradley lounge. In the old days, these two had been poor and undistinguished local hoodlums, and he refused to sit with them in the lounge. They could take him to lunch at Fenton's, he said. Spend a little money on him and see how he was treated with great respect by the maître d'.

Victor Corelli, tall, thin, and swarthy, was dressed like a conservative business man in a dark but ill-fitting suit. Marvin Feldstein, thick-set, well-barbered and perfumed, also had on an expensive but ill-fitting dark suit. When they were about to sit down, Dubuque, fingering the lapel of Corelli's suit, said, "Good cloth, but badly cut, Victor. You boys should get a tailor. You shouldn't get your suits off the rack. People here notice these things." After a pause he said, "Well, what's on your minds?" Corelli, who had a scar from the left corner of his mouth to his ear, told him it had been decided that Dubuque was in an excellent position, with his operation being so well established in his neighborhood, to take over the distribution of drugs. The loan business, and his mortgage-company connection, could come into the organization, too, and they all could make more money. Saying nothing, his face utterly impassive, Dubuque called the waiter and ordered another bottle of wine. He talked to the waiter about the wine. Then, turning to them and shrugging, he said, "I'm not into drugs. I never have been and I'm not starting now. And get this. Big Joe in Montreal knows I don't touch drugs. It's also known that I'm an independent operation. I move against no one. No one moves against me, see? And another thing, and it's the big thing—I don't think you two cut any ice with Big Joe. I think you're on your own, dreaming you'll bring Joe a Christmas present— me—and that'll really surprise him and make you big." Smiling, he had the dessert tray brought to him. While he took his time selecting a pastry, Feldstein and Corelli, not speaking, never took their eyes off him. Finally they nodded to each other; smiling thinly, Corelli said, "This is too bad, Jay."

"For who?" Jay asked in mock surprise. There was a long silence. Shrugging, Dubuque began eating his French pastry with relish. Corelli and Feldstein, watching intently, tried to remain seated in sinister silence. Dubuque finished his dessert. "Oh, I'm blessed with a good appetite," he said. The waiter brought him another cup of coffee. "Good coffee, eh?" he said, but the tension in their silence had become unbearable. Leaning across the table, in little more than a whisper, he said, "Remember little Eddie Roncarelli? Two years ago he tried to move in on me. A clown. A dangerous clown. He came into my office and I had to kick him downstairs. Mind you, the clown came back, saying, 'You forgot one thing, Dubuque. I can get anyone killed, anyone, for a thousand bucks, and I got a thousand.' " Then, as if it had just occurred to him, Dubuque said, "By the way, whatever happened to Roncarelli? Of course, I didn't expect to hear from him again and I didn't."

But they knew what had happened to Roncarelli, a man who had made too many enemies. Roncarelli had been taken out to the country to a farmer's field, and tied up with baling wire in a big roll; some rags were stuffed in it, and the rags were set on fire. The farmer who owned the field, seeing the smoke, got to him while he was still alive. "I wonder where he is now," Dubuque said. "Is he alive or dead? Do you know?"

"See you," Corelli said, standing up suddenly. "Come on, Marvin."

"Yeah, see you, Jay," Feldstein said grimly. "See you for sure."

"I don't think so," Dubuque said, folding his napkin.

Though he had a hunch they were gone out of his life, he walked around warily till he heard they had left town. At the beginning of the next week, on the coldest night so far, he went to the Bradley and then to Mr. Gilhooley's, and he said to Gil, "How about our lady?"

"Our lady? Look, what's with you and our lady?"

"I've got an orderly mind," he said grinning. "I like to see everything in the right place."

"Be my guest."

"Good," he said, pushing the door in the lattice-work open, as only he could, and approaching her. Her eyes were as shrewd and wise as Kitty Cat's, two tables in front of her. It struck him that perhaps she might be there because of the need for some excitement—the danger, the nervous excitement of never knowing what could happen—as much as for any need of money. Under the coat draped around her shoulders, she wore an old-fashioned frilly white blouse and a black skirt. "Remember me?" he asked, sitting down and calling to the waiter.

"I think so," she said.

"Jay Dubuque. At the police station?"

"Of course, I remember."

"Good," he said, expecting her to stop pretending and have a laugh since he was at ease with her on her own turf. "I was in here the other night," he said.

"I saw you."

"You did?"

"What brings you in here? Is it Gil?"

"I've known Gil for years."

"An interesting man, isn't he?" she said, glancing at the lattice grill and Gil's image moving across the big mirror. "They come from all over town, don't they," and the faint accent, the low tone, made her sensually attractive.

"I gather you know Gil," he said. "A well-educated man. He thinks you're an interesting girl."

Glancing again at the latticework, she smiled. "Not to him, really. Gil doesn't need me, Mr. Dubuque."

"Hell, who really needs anybody? Look, it's warm in here. Why don't you take off your coat?"

"I like the feel of it on my shoulders."

There was a thin gold chain with a little antique

cross around her neck, and, leaning closer, he said, "Listen, lady, some guy will rip that right off your neck."

"I don't think so," she said calmly, and while she fingered the cross, he waited for a fold of the coat to fall away from her shoulder so he could see if her breast was full and round, or too small, or even flat. But in spite of the movement of her arm and hand, the coat remained in place.

"Look," he said, "let's see if I've got this right."

"You mean if you've got me right?"

"Right. Let's say a month ago you needed a little money. Money in a hurry."

"Like everybody else."

"And you heard of this place."

"So?" she said, smiling.

"You come here, someone shows you the ropes, and you got the easy money you needed. . . ."

"And so now?"

"Lady, lady," he said earnestly. "I'm saying this joint is not right for you. You got too much class. Get out of this place, Ilona."

"Where should I go?"

"Come on, Ilona. What're you doing here?"

"I'm a whore."

"But a quality whore. A big-buck whore."

"Where should this big-buck whore be?"

"How about your own place? Look, I'm a man who likes to see things in the right place. Your style doesn't go with this place." Then to his amazement he saw in her wise blue eyes the same rejection she had given other solitary men.

"Some place to take calls, eh?" she said disdainfully. "Just a voice on the phone. Don't you understand, Mr. Dubuque, it would be like going into the dark. I don't like the dark. A call, some psychopath waiting. How would I know from his voice? Here a man sits down and I'm looking right at him and I can see what he is."

"Like your Mr. Smiley? You looked right at him."

"All right. I made a mistake."

"No problem, then," he said, letting her see he was accepting her for what she was. The only thing, he went on, was she could make a lot more money at some of the singles bars. The Black Tulip, for example, on a Saturday night. Those affluent people had a lot more money to throw around. She could have some fun, too. Why not have some fun? If a girl suddenly said to a guy, "This is going to cost you a hundred and fifty," well, those guys had it. He talked about the better night places around town and especially the fashionable disco clubs, hoping she would feel closer, get confidential, and come down off her high horse.

"Not for me," she said. "It's not the same thing. It's all something else, isn't it? Rock music and those awful clowns bore me and strobe lights hurt my eyes. And the noise, I get a pain in my chest. Anyway, most of those people just stand around staring at each other. I don't want to go through those motions," and then in a sudden dignified tone, "What do you think I am, Mr. Dubuque?"

He stared at her. He had to laugh. "You're kidding me," he said.

"I beg your pardon."

"Never mind. You've had theatrical experience?"

"No. Why?"

"Maybe in Budapest?"

"I was about three when we left for Austria."

"But you can act, I can tell you act."

"I've never acted."

"You've had acting lessons then."

"Music lessons. That's all."

"Oh, come on," he said grinning, admiring the candor in her eyes. "Now listen . . . listen, please." Seldom in his life had he been so serious, and she saw it, and her face did change. "I know about these things, Ilona. No one knows better than I do. There's a thing in you. Something that gives pleasure to people as soon as they see it. It's a special quality. You're an artist."

"Who told you this?" and she smiled.

"I've seen it working."

"You have?" she said, laughing out loud. "Edmund J. Dubuque, eh?" but her eyes told him he had touched her vanity, some deep core of wild egotism, some fantastic sense of her own special value there on the block, and he went on, more confidently. "I see you somewhere on a stage, in an expensive room . . . in a club. Up there, a somebody."

"Wait a minute, doing what?"

"I don't know, maybe just talking . . . I haven't worked it out yet, or if you could sing a little?"

"You believe this? You really believe it?" and she leaned back.

"I do."

"Mr. Dubuque," she said suddenly, "I don't like your smile."

"My smile?"

"You don't believe what you're telling me because you don't believe in anything."

"Cut it out, Ilona, I tell you I got this hunch about you."

"And you're wrong," she said, but as she eyed him thoughtfully, she looked younger. So he said quickly, "I have connections in this town, Ilona. The right people know me and I keep in touch."

"Yes, I'm sure you do," she said, off by herself, pondering. Then she took a little white handkerchief from a pocket in her skirt and, after touching her nose, began to fold the handkerchief into a square, then into a triangle, while her eyes wandered from the folded handkerchief on the table to the row of tables and the empty chairs in front of her. Only one other girl, a black girl, the Glow-Worm, was there now. Three others were out somewhere.

In the thieves' corner, the pimp Frankie Spagnola, in his dark, conservative executive's suit, was sitting with three quiet little pickpockets, their faces set in expressions they hoped would never be remembered. They were eying Ilona and Dubuque with unconcealed malevolent curiosity, and Dubuque, catching Frankie's eye just as Ilona toyed with the gold cross hanging from the chain on her neck, seemed to see the cross being ripped off. Then he had a familiar feeling, like a chill on his neck, and he looked around warily. He was having one of his hunches, the hunches he trusted, the hunches that had often saved his life. "That's a funny thing," he said, trying to smile. "I must have caught a whiff of something in the air. . . . That guy Smiley throwing you out on the road and all—right then you could have been killed, eh?"

"Well, here I am."

"Each night, any night, you take a chance."

"No one gets killed around here, Mr. Dubuque."

"Those guys you turn down. A whore turning down a guy who's got the money, well, he wants to kill you. Those guys hate you, and if the right one ever gets you on a bed he'll enjoy killing you. And those girls—it's their turf—they won't put up with the way you go on giving stuff away they have a price on. You'll get your face smashed, you'll get maimed." He spoke so quietly and slowly she had to lean closer. "I have these hunches, Ilona. In my business I have to have them or someone would get to me and I'd be dead." Again he tried to smile. "I've seen you in the snow, haven't I? Now I see you beaten up and dead somewhere, and outside it's snowing hard. Isn't it a funny thing that I just saw it? The night of a heavy snow."

Shaken, she shook her head and tried to laugh. "It's incredible," and this time she did laugh. Even so, she looked around the lounge uneasily, and her eyes let him know that while she couldn't make up her mind about him, he would remain in her mind.

"Oh, I get it," she said firmly. "And you're pretty good, Mr. Dubuque. Who wouldn't rather go off with you and get rich than be killed? My God, you are good."

"I'm in the Olympic Trust Building," he said. "Come by my office tomorrow afternoon," and he handed her a card.

"I'll think about it. I'll see."

"I think you will. Let me come to your house."

"No. I live with my parents. They think I'm a secretary working for Secretarial Services. On call, you know, any time."

"I use them every month. Were you ever really with them?"

"I was. I was good, too."

"And if you'd been sent to my office?"

"I'd have been good."

"Tomorrow, then?"

"You know, I half believe you," she said slowly.

"If you don't, I'll come after you. Remember, I know where you live. I had your purse the other night." Taking another business card from his coat pocket, he put it on the table. "Anyway, write down your phone number, Ilona." Then he took another card and began to spell out her name as he wrote: "Ilona. Have I got that right? And Tomory. Is this how you spell it, T-O-M-E-, mmh?"

"No, Tomor . . ." she said. "The accent is on Tom. And with a Y on the end. Not an I."

"That's important?"

"There's a village in Hungary called Tomor. If you spell your name Tomori, it means your father was a carpenter, a tinsmith, or a locksmith or something. But if you are of an old family connected in some way with the nobility, you have a Y, not an I, at the end of the name. Our name is Tomory. My father was an important museum official. Antiquities. National antiquities, you know, Mr. Dubuque." It was fantastic. She was there on the block in this joint, with a burst of laughter coming from the young beer drinkers in leather jackets a few tables away, and yet she was asking with patient dignity that she not be confused with common girls from poor families. "Well, tomorrow afternoon," he said.

"I'll be thinking it over," she said, smiling faintly.

Outside, with loud rock music coming from an open window somewhere near the hotel, he paused before crossing the road and as he pondered he had a slow, wise grin. Ah, she hadn't been so dumb as to try that melting tender stuff on him. She was smart enough to see he didn't need anyone's compassionate interest. Dubuque was a man who exulted in triumphs in his business, whether in loan-sharking or, as it had been in the old days, in extortion. He exulted in his victories over laws he could not accept, never had and never would. But now, suddenly, in spite of his grinning approval of her recognition of the power he had always found in himself, he wished he had seen that melting expression come in her eyes when he was up close to her.

6

IT GOT EVEN COLDER, AND IN THE BRUTAL ZERO
weather a heavy northwest wind blew branches off trees
and at night people everywhere kept off the streets. At
night in such weather, the floodlit white Bradley House,
without the soft veil of snow, looked hard and cold. The
lounge, though, was crowded with neighborhood people
from the old houses that were so hard to heat their pipes
froze, and plumbers couldn't come when called. But
there was always the Bradley lounge. Red-faced and
shivering, they came hurrying into the lounge to relax,
smiling in the wonder of its cozy warmth, a family
warmth, a home. On such nights, even the girls on the
block did not like walking with their clients to the little
tourist home up the street. They were all wearing their
leg-warmers. Yet Rodney Smith, the cabinet minister,
came as usual to the lounge entrance in his big black
limousine, but he, of course, didn't have to leave his car's
warmth. Alfred, his man, had to hop out to select a girl

from the block, who came out grinning at her luck at being able to climb into the heated car. And even in Mr. Gilhooley's, business was slow. The affluent clients on such nights preferred the warmth of their own well-heated homes.

When five days passed and Ilona Tomory did not come to the hotel, Gil assumed it was the weather that had kept her away. But then he began to wonder if Dubuque was to blame. When Gil thought of Dubuque closing in on Ilona, he felt restless and troubled. In his imagination, he saw things happen as if he were seeing her and Dubuque in a story, and this made him remember the days when he had believed he would become a famous story-teller, and how in those days he had received so much encouragement. The poem that had been published in the *Paris Review* had been about the city in the dawn light; the first ones to awake and move around were "undertakers dressed in pink, slinking around to the shrieks of factory whistles". The short story had been about the racetrack, a place he knew, for when he was sixteen he used to hang around the track after dawn, loving the early morning light and the glistening horses working out and drying out, the grooms and clockers at the rail, and the smell of the stable and the smell of coffee. He had thought he would go on writing, but when he became a bartender, moving from city to city, always after better money, his imagination seemed to dry up. He couldn't write. In the bars of Chicago, Las Vegas, Los Angeles, he had known politicians, ball-players, fight managers, whores, jockeys, and brokers: he had thought that all their voices, their faces, their lives, were being stored up in his imagination till the day when they would be characters in his stories. Yet he had never written about them.

Julia, the girl he had known in graduate school, a beauty whose Italian father was a rich builder and contractor, came to live with him in Chicago. They married. She was recklessly extravagant. He loved her for her sense of opulence. But he had to get more money; he had luck, always unbelievable luck, at the racetrack, and he thought the luck came from Julia, who was always at the track with him. He believed it until the day in Chicago when she drove to meet him at the track and her car overturned and she was killed. She left him some money. After that, he let the years pass, getting wise only about putting money aside, and dreaming of going home before he was thirty-six and having this bar called "Mr. Gilhooley's".

Looking through the lattice at the lounge, he had a hunch. It was something like a pricking at the wonder left in him from the old days, a hunch that Ilona, if he got to know her, might be the story he'd been waiting to tell and keep telling. His common sense told him he was a man with responsibilities and should remember that in this hotel they kept track of each other, and besides, he and Mr. Bradley had agreed that no hooker should even be allowed in the bar. That stuff was for the lounge; and he never went into the lounge. His sense of prudence and his business instinct struggled with his need to know enough about Ilona to satisfy his awakening imagination. He saw that he was not free to have her come through that door in the lattice.

And yet he remembered with exasperation how Dubuque had come bursting in from the lounge, pushing open the door, the only one who felt free to do so. Dubuque would do it again, especially now that he had a business interest in Ilona. More than that: he could see Dubuque bringing her into the bar, saying, if questioned,

"What's the door for?" And if Dubuque was seen taking a hooker into the bar, other hookers would follow, and soon there would be no bar for the affluent, window-watching, separated brethren; the whole place would be just one big zoo.

I can't have Dubuque coming in that door, Gil thought grimly. I don't have to take it, and I won't. He may be the club-footed god of this district but there are places in this world where he doesn't belong, and where he can't make his own laws. Imagine him saying he hated to see things in the wrong place—that was a joke. Things were in the right place only when they looked right to him, and if Dubuque ever got big enough to really move in on this hotel, as he planned to take over Ilona, everything would be turned upside down. Merely taking care of his own business, Gil thought, he should have the sense to keep Dubuque out of his bar and out of his life. He told himself he would talk to Mr. Bradley about nailing up the door, closing it permanently, or, better, taking it out altogether before Dubuque could come pushing in with Ilona in her mink coat, sitting down, and smiling as if he believed everyone at the bar would take pleasure in seeing she was now in the right place.

With business so slow these freezing nights, he had lots of time to talk to Mr. Bradley about closing the door, yet he kept putting it off. Leaving Hazel in charge of the bar, he would go up to the Bradley apartment, and sometimes he would have dinner with Mr. Bradley and the twins. In the past few months, Mr. Bradley had asked him to take Ellen, the one who was a little blonder, a little daintier, to a hockey game and to the skating club where she did her figure-skating. Occasionally she would come down to the bar and have a drink and talk to him about horses and football and skiing in Switzerland, and ask him about celebrities he had known in the bars in Vegas. She told him she liked his voice, liked closing her eyes and listening to him.

Gil had always liked J.C. Bradley, who was now a heavy-set man with thin grey hair and a face of such a high color that he looked like a heavy drinker, although Gil had never seen him drunk. He had a slow grin, grinning to himself as if at sixty he had his own secret little joke about life. He had listened when Gil had come back from Vegas with his plan for Mr. Gilhooley's. They became partners. Although Gil never expected to be as rich as Mr. Bradley, he didn't know that he wanted to be, for Mr. Bradley's money seemed to have given him a distorted view of life. No one knew how much money he had, two million, four million, five million. As a young man, he had gone to Harvard to study business administration. All he had got out of it apparently was a sardonic belief that if you had enough money you could live wherever you wanted to live, do what you wanted to do, say what you wanted to say, dress like a bum, refuse to join clubs, and yet be held in high esteem by the whole business community. He had his horses, his farm, and, for his own pleasure, the twins, Ellen and Elsie. They had no money of their own yet, but had always been where money was. When they were young, their mother had made them figure-skating champions, and later they had won ribbons for riding at the horse shows. Since they had always done things together, and won things together, it had not occurred to Mr. Bradley to separate them when he took them so lavishly into his stables and his travels, his home and his bed.

Then, when the weather at last began to moderate, and there was the feel of snow in the air with the ice on the curbs turning to slush, Gil went with Ellen to the skating club. Sitting by himself in the stands, he watched her do her figures, and as she whirled and danced in her little pink ballet skirt, her rhythmic brightness excited him. After the skating, when they had left the rink, nothing was said about where they were going or about Mr. Bradley. He took her to his apartment, which was on Avenue Road near the top of the hill, and they had a drink.

One of the walls of his living room was filled with books, many of them first editions he had picked up in little second-hand bookstores in cities where he had worked. A little shy with her, he wanted to tell her about aspects of his life he had kept hidden, to bring her closer, so he showed her some of the first editions. He talked about Russian and French writers and told her how Turgenev and Flaubert and Tolstoy had seemed to know all the secrets of his own heart and made him restless and eager to write. While he talked he got carried away, because back in his mind he could still see her whirling and dancing, blades flashing, the ice spraying in the wild dancing rhythms of a champion. He told her that in these great writers he had found a truth, a truth that was in him, too. "A reality," he said. "But not just in my own mind. It's out there, too. Outside of my own mind, there is another reality," and then he broke off awkwardly. Smiling, never taking her eyes off him, she pulled off her sweater. "I feel such energy in you, the lovely talking," she said.

Then he helped her undress, taking his time, liking her smile. He made love to her. Afterwards, lying with her eyes closed, and feeling like her bright, happy, straightforward self, she said, "I needed that." She told him she liked his apartment, and they could come there again. They did, twice more, and not once did he, or she, mention Bradley or the nature of her relationship with him, nor did she indicate whether Mr. Bradley preferred her sister, or what it was like for the three of them living together.

At the Bradleys' regular Saturday supper, at which he was always present, Gil believed there would be an exchange of secret glances with Ellen, faint smiles offering new little gifts. Week after week, the same people came to these lavish suppers. The Judge was there, the old family friend; and Tim Feeley, the Irish television producer, a little man who wore a leather peak cap which he never took off, even at the dinner table, and who, according to Bradley, was the best judge of horse flesh in town; and old Tom Staples, the handicapper who had lived his whole life around racetracks, and whom Gil himself always remembered with affection. At sixteen, when Gil was hanging around the track watching the horses working out, he had once said, innocently, to Tom Staples, "When the horses are the same size and the same color, how do you tell them apart, Mr. Staples?" Old Tom had said with disgust, "How do you tell one person from another? Stay by me, boy. You'll learn." All those at the supper loved horses.

On other Saturdays, after the brandy, the Judge had always been prevailed upon to recite poetry, which he could do in the half-mocking style of a grandiloquent nineteenth-century English actor. He knew all the great English poets. Tonight, though he laughed and talked, the Judge was really off by himself with a half-mad loneliness in his eyes, and Bradley was concerned about him. His face a shining pink, he whispered to Gil, "When you get a chance, have a good talk with the Judge, would you, Gil? He likes talking to you. Tells you more than he'll tell me. Thinks you have more imagination. I don't think it's the bad publicity he got over sending that girl to jail for refusing to testify that's really bothering him, it's something else. And look, he said an interesting thing that you might like. He said the law is there for our protection. The law protects. Justice never does. Get him going on that one, eh Gil? I think it's his wife and his dog that have really got him down."

Looking across the table at the Judge, who was drinking more than usual, Gil smiled, and when the Judge in turn smiled, Gil caught a glimpse of Ellen's face. Something about her suddenly jarred him. She was teasing the happy Irish television producer about the little leather hat, trying to get him to take it off. No one could have imagined that Ellen had any personal relationship with him because not a single secret glance had come his way, not even a dreamy expression in her cool, candid blue eyes. Yet a few hours ago she had held him in her arms, straining for, and getting, her satisfaction. The sadness Gil felt was painful. It seemed to him that he had no personal relationship with her, no intimacy at all. In her spirit, she had never left this apartment, never even seen herself in his life, and never would.

And then with a sardonic twist, and some cruel pleasure, he thought, this is a joke. He was trying to keep Ilona out of the bar, make sure she stayed in the zoo; Ilona, whose changing face could tell a man about compassion and tenderness and new waves of life washing around him, was to be kept away. "Good God," he thought. When he left the supper to go down to the bar to be with the eleven o'clock crowd, he did not talk to Bradley about nailing up that door into the lounge.

The bar was crowded, all the regulars were there. It was milder out and snowing a little. Hazel, after asking about the supper, said, "The milder weather brings them all out, doesn't it? Our lady in the coat is back."

"Since when?"

"She's been here all night. And look, I've picked up a little scuttlebutt. Those girls on the block would like to smash up our Hungarian princess."

"Well, they won't. Not around here anyway."

"It's their beef, and she's in it, and they say she takes anything the John leaves on the pillow."

"Any trouble in this hotel and they're all out. They know that, Hazel."

"Not in the hotel. Up some alley, Gil."

7

EVEN THE MOST MENACING AMONG THE BRADLEY'S
customers had come to understand that a truce was
necessary if the lounge was to remain a sanctuary; never
a brawl, never a police raid in the lounge, never an
official visit from a detective. This was why the three
girls from the block, Joyce, Daphne, and Ellie, were
wary of beating up Ilona, even in the washroom. The
place was Ilona's protection. The girls on the block felt
privileged to have been given a chair. They could look
down on the girls working the streets, the girls who
wore skin-tight jeans, or little short skirts, all their
clothes too tight-fitting so that men in passing cars could
see they were prostitutes. The girls on the block, though
they didn't rank as call girls, were well dressed. They
could go shopping or go home or be in public places and
enjoy the freedom of not being noticed.

Daphne was twenty-eight and always jolly, but her
mouth had a bitter twist when she was alone. She had a

seven-year-old son she supported by herself, saving to send the boy to a special school. Unknown to Frankie Spagnola, she had a little bank account. Her friend Ellie, who seemed to be so soft and cuddly, was trying hard to save some money. None of the girls felt as lucky as Ellie did to be able to sit on the block. She had spent six months on the street and knew what it was like to stand on a corner, waving at men in passing cars; when a car stopped, you had to rush at it, with time for only one glance at the face of the man in the car, all your wisdom supposed to be in that glance, the wisdom that would tell you whether this man might kill you or beat you, being full of hate. Then the quick flash of terror, but only a flash, hidden from yourself as you hopped into the car and closed the door. Sometimes the searching glance had failed her; she had been cheated, beaten, robbed, with a knife at her throat. Now Ellie had strange fits of rage which bothered Daphne.

The other girl, Joyce, from the suburbs, was dreamy and nursed a fantasy about opening a beauty parlor. But having made the mistake of letting Frankie keep her money for her, she lay awake at night scheming about how to compel him to give her an accounting.

At nine that evening, the three girls came up the street from the little fast-food restaurant where they ate. The moon had come out, and in the milder air and melting snow, passing cars threw slush up over the curb. One car sprayed slush over Joyce, who screamed at the driver, "You suck-hole idiot. You ape." Ellie and Joyce, in their short, warm, cotton-padded coats and leg-warmers, looked more like coolies than seductive temptresses. Daphne had on a fine three-quarter-length muskrat coat and a man's expensive tweed English cap, which looked quite fashionable with her fur coat. They stopped while Joyce, still cursing, brushed the black slush from her coat, and then Ellie said, "Look, there she is."

Near the lot opposite the hotel, Ilona, in her mink coat, got out of a taxi. "All right. What about now? What do you say?" Ellie said. "Remember, no talk. No talk at all."

"That's right. We gotta say zip," Daphne said. "Don't let her talk."

"No talk," Ellie repeated. "Get her on the mouth, Daphne."

Moving quickly toward Ilona, who was waiting to cross the street, they grabbed her arms, Ellie on one side, Joyce on the other, and hustled her back in among the cars on the lot. Bewildered, carried along, Ilona cried, "What is this?" Though Joyce and Ellie had her arms pinioned, she kept trying to stare into their moonlit faces as they moved through the cars on the lot, their feet sinking into three inches of snow. They marched her to the back of the lot, where they were screened from the street by the abandoned car the bag lady used for sleeping. There, Ilona took on an air, her tall-princess air. "Now take your hands off me at once," she said.

"Cut the sassy shit," Ellie said grimly. "You're moving off our turf."

"You and your nickel-and-dime fucking," Joyce said.

Ilona said nothing.

"All right, smack her, Daphne," Joyce said. "Knock her teeth out."

Drawing back to swing the heavy bag, Daphne wavered. Ilona's eyes were on her. She had always liked Ilona. "Goddamn it," she said.

Pushing Ilona at Daphne, Ellie cried, "Hold on to her, you chicken. I'll do it."

"Ladies, ladies, you're going to regret this," Ilona said, with her high-toned air, not trying to free herself. "Beat me up and it means you're out, back moving your stuff on the street corners. The cops'll come to the hotel and you're out on the street for good."

"The cops, you fancy showboating bitch," Ellie said.

"Don't be a fool, Ellie," and Daphne grabbed Ellie's arm.

"Shut your face, Daphne."

"If the cops come around, Frankie'll kick the shit out of us."

"Okay," Ellie said finally. "You're going to move your ass off our turf, lady, or get dumped on the highway. Just wait," and, leading Joyce and Daphne through the cars to the street, she complained, "I said, don't let her talk, and you let her talk, Daphne."

"No, you did, Ellie."

"I kept saying shut up, so I could whack her." They crossed the street to the lounge, with Daphne looking back at Ilona, who was at the curb, watching them and trying to relax and stop trembling.

"Daphne," Ilona called.

"What?"

"Come here, Daphne."

"What for?"

"Just a minute." Daphne said something to Ellie and pointed at Ilona, and Ellie cursed as Daphne shook her head and then crossed the road again and said, "Look, the fact is I think I've always looked up to you."

"What I want to know, Daphne, is was this personal?"

"Nothing personal," she said. "You're screwing up our turf."

"Daphne, have a coffee with me?"

"A coffee?" Daphne said, surprised.

"Whenever you want."

"Where?"

"Wherever you want."

"Not around here," Daphne said. "I know a place on Yonge." And then, tongue-tied and shy, but not understanding why, she waited, frowning, and with a sudden eager smile she said, "Yeah, and I'd like to bring my little boy along. You want to meet my kid? He ain't got much sophisticated smarts but he's a great kid. Okay?" She hurried back to the lounge door and then looked back. Ilona, who had remained at the curb staring at the white floodlit hotel, took a step off the curb, then slowly drew back, still staring at the hotel. It was as if she had been touched by some overwhelming dread of what was in store for her there and could not move toward the lounge till she overcame the dread.

8

WHILE ILONA WATCHED THE HOTEL ENTRANCE AND wondered if this was the night when she should turn away, Dubuque was taking it easy in his own home with his wife. During the three days of brutally cold weather when Ilona had not been seen at the hotel, he had expected each day to have her appear at his office. When she didn't come, he wasn't discouraged. He blamed the weather, and he thought, too, that she might have caught a glimpse of the fate awaiting her, and had seen it as he himself had seen it, or felt it. When he had talked to her, the shadow in her face told him she had been shaken, even if just for the moment. While waiting for some word about her from the hotel, he went about his own business, organizing a protective association for bookies. Too many were being raided, and a large fund had to be raised to pay for consistent tip-offs on the raids.

But tonight neither the bookies nor Ilona were on his mind. He loved these quiet evenings at home, with

Michelle gossiping about the neighbors while he in his slippers and Cardin sweater read the dictionary. Each night, no matter what was happening, before going to bed he went over four pages, savoring the words that were strange, getting the exact meaning of each big word and its pronunciation. Long ago, he had learned from his crazy father that words could become deadly weapons when used on illiterate people. His wife, having been a nurse in training, talked well with a kind of lazy good-humored drawl. There was a warmth and ease in the way she used words. He hadn't told her about his interest in Ilona: he really believed Ilona was just a property, a business interest.

Michelle was telling him now that the neighbors were keeping after her, the wives inviting her into their homes, always asking questions and hoping to be asked to visit the Dubuque house. One of these wives was an editor on a woman's magazine, another had a husband who was a television producer. Grinning at his wife, Dubuque put down the dictionary, got up and touched her head fondly, seeing her as the mother of his child. He wanted to have a family and it had troubled him that he had found it so hard to make such a motherly woman pregnant, and last week he was overjoyed when she whispered to him that they would have a child. As he touched her head, his smile let her know how pleased he was with her, but then there was a knock on the door.

"At this hour? Who the hell is this?" he grumbled, going to the door. It was Frankie Spagnola, his expensive black overcoat hanging open so he could display his three-piece suit.

"Well, how's Da Boot?" Frankie asked, leaning back against the wrought-iron railing, his black hair shining under the light hanging over the entrance.

"Spagnola . . . well . . ." Dubuque said. Outraged that this man had come to his home, but keeping his voice down, Dubuque closed the door behind him and stepped out to the stoop in his sweater and slippers. It was cold out but not freezing, and there was a lot of slush on the pathway up to the stoop. Frankie's car was parked at the curb in front of the house—a nice big black car.

Dubuque had known Frankie for years. He had watched him grow from a skinny kid into a man who had dreamed of becoming the middle-weight champion of the world, yet couldn't train faithfully. Managers had found him hard to handle, and besides, fast and all as he was, he had no punch. After his retirement he had tried being a burglar, and with some success: he had only been jailed once, and not for burglary, but for possession of burglars' tools. Three years ago he had seduced a high school girl, a runaway, and put her out to work for him. Now Frankie thought of himself as the only pimp in town who had any class.

While Frankie stood on the stoop brushing away a few drops of water that had fallen on his head from the snow on the wrought-iron casing around the light, Dubuque said quietly, "The name is Dubuque," feeling that his wife and all the respectable wives on the street were watching him. "Why do you come to my house?"

"Aren't you going to ask me in?"

"Like hell I am. What do you want?"

"Okay, Jay," he said, shrugging. "Just one word."

"Be quick about it. I'm getting cold."

"That girl, Ilona."

"Don't bother me, Frankie."

"I know you think you have the edge around here," Spagnola said. "I'm not sure how big you are. But I saw you talking to the Hungarian. I know you're trying to suck her into something. So look, she's my action, Dubuque. I've been nursing her along. So butt."

"Bullshit, Frankie."

"Nursing her, just like a daddy, letting her play the amateur on the girls' turf. But you want to use her, talk to me first."

"You first?" Dubuque said, pondering before shaking his head gravely. "This is business, right? Just a little business. I can tell it's just business."

"You can tell what?"

"I can tell from the suit you got on. The expensive suit, the threads," and he brushed open one fold of Frankie's coat. "If I'd known you were coming, I would have put on my own three-piece suit. Businessmen, eh Frankie?"

"Fucking my head, eh? Well, I take care of my business."

"So do I," Dubuque said, his hand on Frankie's shoulder.

Suddenly he let his hand slip to the back of the collar of the open coat, and he jerked the coat down Spagnola's back, spinning him around, his arms pinned to his sides by the coat; then, letting go of the coat, Dubuque punched him hard on the nose, sending him in a stutter-step down the steps, where he sprawled in the slush, blood trickling from his nose. Hopping down the steps in his slippers and nearly tripping, Dubuque shouted, "Slime! Don't come around here again. Don't you dare come near this house, you cheap little mother-fucking pimp. And hands off the girl, or you'll get your legs broken." Forgetting that he had his slippers on and not the heavy boot, he kicked Frankie savagely in the ribs and then kicked him again, hurting and numbing his club foot. While he limped around, Frankie on his knees, eying the distance to his car, said, "Okay! Okay for now, big man," and he got up, wiping the slush from his coat. "But she'll work for me. She'll have to."

"Take off, you bastard, run."

"You'll get your feet wet," Frankie said, backing toward his car. "I tell you this, the ladies don't like this Ilona, it's bad for business. They'll tie a can to her, Dubuque. You know how they can fix a woman."

As Dubuque, his feet soaking and cold in the slush, lunged after him, Frankie got to the safety of his car. Breathing hard, Dubuque went into his house. His wife said, "Who was that?"

"Some creep I didn't like who wanted a handout and got insulting. I had to chase him," and he hurried into the bedroom to change his wet socks before she noticed them. In the bedroom, gently massaging the toes of his club foot, he wondered if he had broken the big one. Suddenly, he said to himself, "Goddamn it! That pig-headed Hungarian! I told her. I told her," and he felt vindicated in his judgment of what would happen to Ilona Tomory in the Bradley lounge. It would happen even though Spagnola himself would be afraid to beat her. But Frankie's ladies would; somebody would slash her, and then . . . no good to me or anyone else, Dubuque thought.

When he went to bed with his wife, he fell into a deep sleep that lasted till four in the morning. Then, waking suddenly, he found himself thinking of Spagnola. The man's audacity in coming to the house still astonished him. He couldn't sleep. Lying in the dark, he wondered if Ilona Tomory, after the three cold days, had been drawn back to the lounge, and if she had been there tonight when Frankie Spagnola returned. Then he asked himself what had awakened him so suddenly. Immediately he became uneasy, and as the uneasiness deepened, he remembered his hunches—his strange visionary gift that was like a compensation for his club foot and the recent hunch that she would be found lying still and cold somewhere some night it would be snowing steadily, snowing all night long.

Moving carefully so as not to disturb his sleeping wife, he slid out of bed and hurried to the window and looked out. No snow. None at all! A mild, clear night, and for the first time in a week the night clouds were breaking up, with a clear, bright moon riding across the great, inky widening seas.

(9)

IT HAD BEEN A GOOD NIGHT AT THE HOTEL. THE lounge was crowded. Ilona, having finally decided to come in, was at her table, and the ladies of the block threw unbelieving belligerent glances at her, then tried to get the eye of Frankie Spagnola, who had returned and was in his chair in the thieves' corner. Off by himself, concentrating, Frankie did not move towards his girls or Ilona. He knew that if he made one false turn, he would be thrown out and kept out. So, he sat back, trying to look stern.

In Mr. Gilhooley's bar, a radio and television satirist who had lost both his shows was trying out new routines on two college boys and their Rosedale girls. They were a little giddy because three horse-players who had just come back from Santa Anita, where they'd had fantastic luck, had ordered champagne for everyone. Judge Gibbons was there, too, off by himself at the curved end of the bar. At last he was having his long talk with Gil.

Whenever someone called Gil, Hazel was there to help him. Those at the bar who knew the Judge and respected him did not want to interrupt.

Around town, there were distinguished jurists, old classmates and men in trust companies who would have been flattered and moved if Judge Gibbons had sat with them in one of their clubs, trying to explain why he was so upset by the publicity that had followed his jailing of the young woman for thirty days for contempt. He seemed to believe that his old admiring friends, because of the lives they led, could not understand the root of his loneliness and his disappointment in himself. At a private dinner, or a legal conference, these friends liked to hear him talk, believing he brought all of English literature and all of English history to them. He knew both subjects well, and had become a little ponderous and pontifical. No one could name an historical work he hadn't read. One jurist, trying to catch him, said, "I came across something the other night I'm sure you haven't read. It was in my grandfather's library—Machiavelli's history of the rise of Florence."

"Ah, yes, I know it well. I know all of Machiavelli," he said. His colleague simply didn't believe him, but it was true. The Judge had also written a much-admired pamphlet on legal jargon, and on legal barbarisms in the use of the language. He had a son at Oxford.

But Gil had discovered that the Judge knew little or nothing about the literature of the Russians or the French, only their history. The Judge's imagination seemed to be wholly English. "All right, Gil," he once said, "you tell me about your Dostoevski and I'll tell you about Trollope." But talking to Gil had always made him feel young, and he used to wonder if it was too late for him to enlarge his imagination. "It's a strange thing," he said once to Gil, "but when I get talking to you, catching your fanciful mode of thought, I feel closer to you than I do to my own son, though I love him very much."

Sitting at the end of the bar, he peered through the lattice at the crowded lounge and his face kept changing as if something or someone in there held his interest. Then he would seem to be cut off by himself, reflecting. After looking again he grew troubled and turned away.

When Gil returned, the Judge said, "I think this is what I want to talk about, Gil. You know they say many a jurist's opinions or attitudes depend on what he had for breakfast, or some trouble he had with his own son. Well, there are things happening in a man's life, maybe the real things, that he can't ever feel safe in telling, eh Gil?" With an embarrassed little shrug, he went on, "You know my wife suffers with terrible arthritis, don't you?"

Frowning, trying to understand this part of the story, he told how it became a passion with him to look after his ailing wife and make her comfortable. He hated to see her suffer. If he was in the big house and heard her groan, no matter what room he was in he would run to her. For a month she would be bedridden, hardly able to move on the bed, and then for another month she would be able to get around the house with a cane and be very much like herself, mistress of the home. It was her domain. Everything that happened in the house was under her control and supervision. Encouraging her to have this view, he believed he was defeating the crippling arthritis, or at least holding it in check. She read a lot, and until her fingers got badly crippled, she used to paint. He got two wheelchairs, one for the house that she could operate herself, and one for the street, in which he used to push her around on long walks through the neighborhood. When she had friends to the house, she used her motorized chair. Since she never complained, he thought she had the sweetness of a saint.

Three years ago he had been given a dog, a giant French poodle, only a month old, and the dog trotted along beside him when he wheeled his wife around. The neighbors got used to seeing them coming along the street after dinner in the summers, then in twilight as the autumn came on, and then into the winter, when his wife was bundled up. Some of the neighbors thought the chair was too heavy for a man of sixty. It was a terrible hardship, they said. But he grew to like it; it grew on him, first the business of coaxing her to get into the chair, then making her so comfortable she would smile and begin to talk and sound like herself. Later in the evening, when he had got his wife into a comfortable position in bed, he would take Bruno, the big black poodle, for a walk around the neighborhood, talking to the dog, feeling that the day had been a good one, and that this was the time for playful relaxation.

For five years he had had no sexual relations with his wife. Lovemaking would have been too painful for her. Yet he had felt that they had handled it well: sexual intimacy denied gave dignity and strength to their lives, and indeed became part of that passion he had developed for trying to overcome her suffering.

In his law office, he had a first-class legal secretary who needed an assistant. She brought in a young woman of thirty with jet-black hair and soft brown eyes, who came to admire him. She kept asking him what she should read, and in her turn brought him some books of poetry and offered to come to the house and take his wife for a walk in the wheelchair. She had very fine skin, very fine hair, too, and a smile that was more like a grin, a sudden flash of life. In the years of his marriage, he hadn't got involved with any other woman. He had come to believe that desire for women had been lost in the almost pleasurable concern and labor of looking after his wife.

Yet he had let the girl take him to her apartment for a drink, and when they had the drink he went to bed with her. In the next month there were more visits to the apartment and the girl became very emotional about him. She laughed a lot, but cried a lot, too, and when he was out of town she would telephone just to hear his voice. She even brought legal papers to the house for him to sign, just to be in the house and see his crippled wife. One day, calling his office, his wife got the girl on the phone and seemed to learn something talking to her, learn by an instinctive recognition of an emotion, and perhaps by a recollection of what she had seen in the girl's face when she came to the house, or perhaps by that heightened awareness the disabled have when they feel threatened. She asked him, "What about this girl? Are you going to tell me about this girl?"

The pain in her grey eyes made it hard for him to speak, and, sitting down beside her, waiting while the shame grew in him, he then said finally, "At my age! Yes," and struggled to find some dignity, which he knew could only come if he told the truth, if he told how he had almost forgotten about the temptations of the flesh, if he told that he had never touched another woman until this girl came along. Indeed, he had always imagined that he found a sensual and spiritual satisfaction in caring for and protecting his wife. It had never been a hardship. It had been a pleasure, and he would have been lost and lonely without this pleasure. "I've made an old fool of myself," he said. "The girl will leave the office and leave my life."

As she looked at him steadily, he thought she had weighed and been moved by his years of devotion when she couldn't be a woman to him, for she said gently, "I understand, my husband, oh, I understand." And that night, after he had helped her get comfortable in her bed, and had brought her the evening newspaper to read, he took the big poodle out for their walk and talked to him, repeating again and again, "Confession is good for the soul. I never would have believed it. Yet it feels so good, so very good, and I am myself again."

His wife's grace began to provoke in him a profound admiration. She never mentioned the girl again. It seemed to him that she had said all a superior woman needed to say with her "I understand." A month passed. Using her cane, she moved around the house more freely. He hoped for some kind of magical remission. Then, one day she said to him, "Bruno has become so much your dog, John. He misses you terribly all day long and I can't handle him."

"You don't have to handle him," he said. "He'll sleep. Let him sleep."

"He's so big, and the other day he almost knocked me over, I could have broken my hip."

"But you didn't break your hip," he said.

"You don't know how Bruno runs around the house. He actually knocked the cane out of my hand. He leaps at me now as he leaps at you."

"Oh, come on, I've never seen him leap at you," he said.

"John, do me a favor please."

"What?" he said.

"Get rid of Bruno."

"I can't."

"Of course you can," she said gently. "He's just a dog. You'll have to get rid of him, because I can't look after him."

"Ah, I see," he said, and as she smiled, he felt stricken, then humiliated, the humiliation becoming so intense he could only stare in a dumb disappointment. He had actually believed she had had a saintly tolerance when she recognized that he had yielded to a need she herself couldn't satisfy. As she smiled very gently, her eyes told him she believed he would recognize there was a certain equity in having him suffer some loss, a rough justice. It was little to ask, since she could sue him for divorce, and cause a scandal that he, as a member of the judiciary, couldn't stand. Looking around the room, he struggled desperately to find the right words. He looked at the French paintings hanging on the walls of the room while she waited and waited for him to speak. She owned the paintings.

Finally he said, "That big elegant poodle. Where is he?" and again he looked all around. "I remember the first time Bruno ever saw the snow," he said. Bruno had been just four months old at the time of the year's first snowfall. He had taken him out and the dog, pausing on the path to the house, looked up at the snow coming down so heavily and melting on his fur; snow, a new wonder in his world of expanding wonders. Circling slowly, the dog looked up at him. "Then he dashed across the road to our neighbors' lawn where the snow was much thicker," he said to her, "and then he started hurling himself around in short circles. Sometimes he jumped up in the air like a ballet dancer, his open mouth catching the snowflakes, and then with a last look around he came trotting sedately back to me." That was all he said to her. Saying nothing, she swung her wheelchair around and left him.

"You can see, Gil, that the dog had to go," the Judge said, shrugging. "I had a friend, a lawyer who had a farm about forty miles away, who agreed to take him."

Irons, the television satirist near the other end of the bar, called Gil.

"Just a minute," Gil said to the Judge. But after taking a few steps, he looked back; the Judge, having swung around on his stool, a bitter twist to his mouth, was staring morosely through the lattice, staring intently into the crowded lounge, a lonely man held rapt. Five minutes later he said to Gil, "As I was saying, or as I was just thinking, you can't talk to an animal every night for five years without developing a language, an intimacy. In its language, the animal, if he is close to you, is never devious, the trust is there, the bond is there forever. Have you noticed this, Gil?"

"It's the same with some people," Gil said.

"So it is, Gil. Well, when a doctor decided to take my wife to a nursing home to work some newfangled cure on her arthritis, I was alone in the house, and at night when I would have walked Bruno I felt lonely."

"Perfectly natural," Gil said.

"The thing was that even though I was disappointed in my wife, I also felt, to my astonishment, that I had never known much about her, and somehow I was terribly disappointed in myself, too. I knew I had lost all authority in the house, and had become a man without any authority in his real life. Authority! Well, about that girl I threw in jail for contempt of court . . ."

"Judge, was it contempt for the law or respect for her own heart?" Gil asked.

"It has become a matter of conscience for me now," the Judge said earnestly, reddening. "I'll have to get her out of that jail. The victim in jail, the aggressor free— it's the law, but it's not justice. But I'm telling you how I felt. A lonely, disappointed man who had discovered he no longer had any authority in his own house. Something flared out of me. The only place where I had any authority was my own court. Right? It was not like me, Gil. Look, someone is calling you. I'm monopolizing you. . . ."

Gil hadn't liked the deep sigh that came from the Judge as he turned away from him, looking into the lounge, but when he came back to the end of the bar, the Judge had gone. About three-quarters of an hour later, Hazel, who had gone out to the lobby to get some cigarettes from the tobacco stand near the entrance, came back smiling. "Well, what do you know!" she said.

"Well, what do I know?"

"The Judge and our lady."

"What?"

"He must have been sitting in that chair near the tobacco stand. When she returned he must have spoken to her. When I saw them, she had that smile on her face and they were going out together."

10

ALL NEXT DAY THERE WERE WEATHER WARNINGS FOR those intending to travel; great snowstorms moving up the eastern seaboard had turned inward; the weathermen predicted a ten-inch snowfall. Yet snow didn't come till ten in the evening; then it came in a thin, fine, hardly noticeable fall almost like rain, and with no swirling wind. It kept on streaming down all through the night, and by morning the snowploughs couldn't handle it. By eight in the morning, when the storm had ended, a thin sunlight lightening the sky fell on a snowbound, almost motionless white city. Taxicabs could not move on the side streets, nor could morning newspapers be delivered.

The television news was all about power failures, accidents on highways, and reckless motorists who tried to keep driving though they couldn't see, and about schools being closed for the day. Then, in a final item, after some international stories, a murder was reported;

last night a woman had been killed in a shabby little tourist home up the street from the Bradley. Though the woman's name was withheld until her immediate relatives could be notified, there was a description: she was taller than average, had light brown hair, and wore some kind of fur coat. Robbery had not been involved, it was clear, for the woman's purse, the contents untouched, had been left in the room.

The reporter had the night clerk, Harold Hines, on tape; he was grey-haired and middle-aged and looked as if he never got enough sleep, and had long ago lost his capacity for excitement. Harold Hines said he couldn't remember the man who had come in with the girl. He wouldn't have paid much attention, anyway. The truth was, he had been dozing, and hadn't seen the man at all, and had assumed they had gone upstairs to room no. 5. At this point Harold Hines made one stormy protest. It was not fair to say he didn't care what happened to these girls after they had paid for the room. As a family man himself, with three daughters, he had been so concerned about all these girls that he had worked out a safety system for them: a girl being beaten or in pain needed only to swing her arm and knock the telephone off the hook and the buzzing switchboard told him to grab his heavy Irish blackthorn and go running up the stairs.

But he had heard no cries, no sound of a struggle, no sound of footsteps running down the stairs. Of course, the stairs were heavily carpeted, a brown carpeting badly worn and torn at the edge of the lifts, said the reporter who covered the story, old carpeting that matched the walls, done in faded, blotched oatmeal paper. Harold Hines said that when he heard the buzzing on the switchboard he had gone leaping up the stairs, in spite of the sudden sharp pain in his arm and chest from angina.

He couldn't say how long he had been dozing before he heard the buzzing. From the top of the stairs he saw the open door, no. 5, a small, dingy unit, everything from carpet to walls to bedcover faded and drab. There was a sink and a chair. Her purse was on the chair.

As soon as he reached the open door, Harold Hines screamed. The tall girl with the light-brown hair stood naked in the middle of the room, her back to him. A long knife stuck out of her back below the shoulder blades. Blood streamed down to her hips. While he yelled, gaping at her, she sank to the floor. He ran down the stairs and called the ambulance, then the police, and all he could tell the police was that he hardly knew this girl.

As he listened to the radio Mr. Bradley was having breakfast in bed. It was served playfully by the twins, who enjoyed vying with each other, making a game out of Mr. Bradley while he made a game of them, too, a game the three played with ingenuity and laughter. To-morrow, Mr. Bradley was having the steel brace removed from the broken leg that had not healed properly. The twins had agreed with him that in a week they should leave for Florida and a month in the sun. Suddenly he called sharply, "Ellen, please, take the tray," and sat up in bed listening to the story of the girl murdered in the tourist home up the street. He cursed softly. The high color left his cheeks. "One of those lousy little girls from the lounge," he said. "This kind of publicity I won't stand for. It's not amusing. It's ruinous." The girls, afraid of him when he was in this mood, said nothing.

Getting out of bed, he limped quickly to the bedroom telephone and called his lawyer, once a partner of Judge Gibbons. He called him at home without apology.

His voice harsh, Mr. Bradley told the lawyer that no matter the cost, that girl was not to be linked in any way with the Bradley in the newspapers or on the air. "This is what money is for," he said. "I'll owe you one," and he hung up abruptly.

Dubuque, too, having breakfast with Michelle and listening to the news, complained that it might be all day before the snowploughs came along his street. The light coming through the window greenery mellowed the knotty-pine panelling of the breakfast nook, putting a glow on Michelle's neck and throat. As she moved about the spotless kitchen, the strong overhead kitchen light put a sheen on her pretty silken housecoat. Her round, sweet face always gave Dubuque a sense of well-being that usually lasted all day. "You know our neighbor, the editor, Mrs. Brigham?" she said. "Well, she's a strange one. When we've come home sometimes at two in the morning I've seen her sitting in the dark at her front window, just watching the lighted windows across the street. I even waved to her once. Yesterday I asked her why she did it, and with that mysterious smile of hers she said, 'I light my life through other people's windows because my house is dark.' Wasn't that clever?" Not hearing a word, Dubuque listened intently to Harold Hines, the night clerk, telling how a tall girl in some kind of fur coat had died in room 5.

Dubuque walked slowly out of the kitchen to the front room and stood looking out at the unbroken snow-covered street. He had a feeling he couldn't cope with for a moment. All night long it had been snowing, and then, just as he had foreseen it, a girl was lying stiff in a room while it snowed hard outside. "Well, there it is, just like I told her," he said aloud. He could only stare at the snow, feeling larger than he ever thought he was, a little bit frightened by this clear evidence of his visionary power.

Gil hadn't been able to finish his breakfast. Bradley phoned and told him that no one at the hotel, no one having any connection with the hotel, was to show any interest in the girl. No sooner had Gil finished talking to Bradley than the telephone in his apartment rang again. Judge Gibbons said it was absolutely necessary that they talk. Distraught, the Judge said that if the girl was Ilona—and he was sure it was Ilona—and if her purse, with his card in it, had been found . . . "I've got a man digging a path from the house to the street," he said. "The snowplough has been along the street. If I can get a taxi, I'll be there in half an hour."

But it was two hours before he arrived, wearing heavy rubber boots, a blue turtleneck sweater, and a camel's-hair jacket. His thick silvery hair, usually combed so carefully, was down around his ears. Sitting in the chair where Ellen had sat, and drinking a cup of coffee, he tried to maintain his dignity while apparently struggling against a conviction that he was doomed to a ruinous disgrace for some reason he did not understand. "I got involved with Ilona," he said.

"I know," Gil said.

"How did you know?"

"You were seen talking to her in the lobby, then going out with her."

"Everything is seen, isn't it? And now this, and the purse." As he sighed, his mouth took a bitter twist. "While I talked to you at the bar I looked through that grill from time to time. I saw her. I had seen her at other times, Gil. Anyway, I saw her go out. When I left you, I was haunted by something comforting, something soothing and enchanting I had seen come into her face. I don't know. I needed what I saw, Gil. And then, acting blindly, foolishly, I left the bar, then made my way to the hotel lobby and waited. When she returned, I spoke to her. While she stood contemplating me, a man of sixty, lonely and worried about what was happening in his life, I said simply, 'Would you come home with me for a while?' For a few moments she said nothing, maybe getting the hang of me, and I felt she knew who I was. I don't know, maybe she didn't care who I was. Smiling slowly, she said, 'Of course, I will,' and took my arm. Saying nothing more to each other we went out to my car and drove to my home."

The Judge said that when he took her upstairs to his library, which was next to the bedroom, he became flustered because she saw that he was in unfamiliar circumstances, and was trying to behave conventionally. She was amused. While he got a tray, a bottle of brandy, and some glasses, she wandered around the library, glancing at the books with real curiosity. Going into the bedroom, he turned on the lights and stared at the bed. When he returned to the library, he could see that she had poured the drinks. They touched glasses. When she laughed so easily, it was as if she expected him to lead her into the bedroom, or as if she would simply say, "Well, let's get to it."

Instead, glass in hand, she wandered over to the bookshelf to stand before the little section devoted to English poetry, and after a few moments of scrutiny she pulled from the shelf a thin volume. By its thinness and color he knew what it was: *A Shropshire Lad* by A.E. Housman. Watching her flick idly through the book, he believed she was waiting impatiently for him to take her into the bedroom. His heart began to pound. He could neither speak nor take his eyes off her. He felt like a bewildered high school boy. Turning to him, the little book in her hand, she said gently, "You don't want to go to bed with me."

"I want you."

"But not really to go to bed with me," she said with a faint smile. She had on a very pale mauve-colored cashmere sweater and a brown tweed skirt. Still smiling, she pulled the sweater over her head. There was no brassiere underneath the sweater. Naked to the waist, she let him look at her. Leaving her skirt on, she sat down. Then, leaning back on the pillow, she opened the book, turning one page, then another, sometimes frowning while the floor lamp shone on her breasts, and on the nipples and on her neck. "These are like songs, aren't they?" she asked. She was reading 'Summertime on Bredon', reading it aloud but a bit awkwardly. She would lower the book, smile, nod, and he would nod. And the changing expressions in her face touched him with a tenderness and an excitement he had never known before. The excitement was not lust. It was more like elation. He knew that a man could believe in anything he wanted to believe, and that this capacity had caused so much trouble in the world, but there was one rapt moment, watching her, when he caught a glimpse of a hidden wonder in life, an intimation, too, that real life was elsewhere.

He didn't know how long she remained half-naked on the couch. But, having kept her wristwatch on, she now looked at it, put the book down on the end table, got up, stretched luxuriously, and pulled on her sweater. While he stood beside her, she took his head in her hands and kissed him delicately yet intimately on the mouth. Fumbling his words, he said, "Wait." Going to the desk, he got one of his cards, wrote down his phone number, and put the card in her purse. He had at least a hundred dollars in his wallet, and he slipped the money into her purse. Helping with her coat, he said, "I can't go after you. Can you phone me? There must be another night. Will you? You must."

"I may at that. I like you. I like it here," she said. "Can you get me a cab?"

"That's the way it was, Gil," the Judge said. "But it's that damned purse. If it's her purse they've got . . ." Looking at Gil, pleading for support in his profound protest, he spoke of the dreadful ironic unfairness of life; the one night that had been a beautiful, consoling, and ever-to-be-remembered sweet experience could be the night that ruined his reputation, a judge who consorted with whores.

11

BY THIS TIME THE POLICE HAD NOTIFIED THE DEAD girl's next of kin. They had no trouble identifying her. There were cards in her purse saying that in the event of an accident her mother, in St. Catharines some forty miles away, and Frankie Spagnola should be notified. Frankie gave the news to the girls at the lounge, and one of the waiters, who kept an eye on things for Dubuque, telephoned and told him Daphne was the girl. Later, in the evening newspaper, Daphne was identified as the mother of a seven-year-old son. No mention was made of the Bradley House.

The discovery that he had been wrong in his vision of a death on a snowy night relieved and yet baffled Dubuque. In fairness to him, the bafflement did not spoil his sense of relief, and soon he was able to tell himself that his picture of a girl lying dead while it snowed had been accurate, which meant that his hunches could indeed sometimes have a visionary power. In naming the girl, he had been wrong; but that was merely interpretation, and quite aside from the power of the hunch. He felt gratitude to Daphne and felt very sentimental about her. It was almost as if he recognized that she had agreed to take the place of the girl he had seen in his vision, and so he knew something should be done for her.

When the snowplough cleared his street and he could get out of the house, he went to his office and put in a phone call to his mortgage company, whose office was on the same floor. Then he dropped in on them himself, talked to their lawyer, wrote a cheque for a thousand dollars, and told the lawyer he was to get it to Daphne's mother, a gift for Daphne's son.

From his office window, he could see out over the roofs of smaller buildings to his old neighborhood, where the ramshackle house in which he had been born still stood. Often, when he stood at the window, he was a little awed that he had become so powerful and successful so quickly. Yet he had known when he was a boy that some day he would have this power. All afternoon he felt strangely expectant and confident. When finally he heard someone at the office door, he stood up. Here she comes, he thought. It was only a Salvation Army girl asking for a donation. Yet it was nearly five o'clock.

To pass a little more time, he picked up the phone and called the Cookie Lady, a respectable middle-aged married woman now, who still lived in the old neighborhood. After a few minutes of good amusing conversation, he said, "It must be the weather. I'm feeling sentimental," and he told her he was sending her two hundred dollars. He wanted her to pick out a destitute family in the neighborhood, buy them a beautiful dinner with all the fixings and some small gifts for the children, and say simply that he was their friend and they were his people. He told her he wanted her to do this because he did not trust the judgment of any minister or priest or welfare worker. "Those guys get everything wrong," he said.

Having done this, he looked again at his watch, grabbed his coat and hat, hurried out to his car, drove east over the river as far as the jail, then turned up the avenue that skirted the park and ravine. By this time it was snowing quite heavily. Down in the park there was the great stretch of flat land where he had played when he was a kid, snow-covered now, flat and bleak and dead, and far behind it in the falling snow rose the hills with the roofs of affluent homes above the bare trees, all grey and cold in the descending darkness and falling snow. In the summertime, "the flats" had been brilliantly green. One summer night when he was sixteen, right there in the middle of the field where they felt secure, since any figure approaching in the moonlight could be seen from a hundred yards away, he had made it with a girl he hardly knew. He had picked her up in the park. He had been wearing his mother's ring, a gold ring with an emerald which he had discovered in a bureau drawer, the only valuable thing his mother had kept and treasured; and he had liked having it on his own finger. But the girl, after he had made it with her, started to cry. "Let me wear that ring tonight," she pleaded, "I'll feel better," and he let her wear it.

But when he got home, he was so shaken that he had let her keep the ring that he couldn't sleep, and couldn't understand how he could have been such a fool as to have believed her when she said, "I'll bring it here tomorrow night." He wasn't even sure where the girl lived. His mother's ring! He had been such a fool. At the same hour the next night, he was there in the park, waiting, and feeling like a fool for waiting. He was sure he would never see her again. When he saw her coming out of the shadows, he was stunned, almost afraid of her, then shy. She gave him back the ring, which his own wife now wore on her little finger.

Driving along now, he was trying to remember the name of that girl who was there in his mind, her face, her voice, but he couldn't remember her name. It became important to him that he try to remember the name before he got to Ilona Tomory's street. Elsa. Jean, Hazel, Eva. Something like Eva. He almost had it. But then he came to Ilona's street, where all the houses looked alike, small and cheap, a hundred houses with the same verandas. He remembered the address, having seen it in her purse that first night when he had picked up the contents of her purse in the snow. In the thick falling snow, he couldn't make out the numbers on the houses. It was almost dark. Getting out, he tried two houses. His footsteps broke the first path in the snow to her house. She came to the door. "Oh," she said. "So it's you."

"I was sure I would see you today, Ilona. I mean after what happened to Daphne."

"Poor Daphne. Oh dear God."

"Well, it was just like I said it would be."

"What? Oh no. Not quite."

"Daphne instead of you."

"So, you made a mistake?"

"No mistake, Ilona. It's in the cards, if you go back to the hotel. You can't."

"I don't know. Oh, I don't know. Daphne had a little son."

"A seven-year-old kid, they say. Something should be done for that kid."

"Like what?"

"For one thing, a collection in the lounge. Look, I can put out the word that a decent collection will be taken as a favor and appreciated by me. You keep out of it. I know you can't bear to go back there now. And as I told you, I know something that suits you better." He looked around. "Can we talk?"

"Well, now that you're here, I suppose so. Come in." And then he was in a narrow hall with a narrow staircase, the staircase completely covered with a shaggy, thick, rich taupe-shaded Indian carpet, and there was a thick Oriental rug in the hall. The walls were done with some kind of leathery, heavy, embossed paper that looked like antique carving, and in a beautiful vase on a little table stood a bunch of yellow roses. But for a moment, seeing none of these things, he grinned with satisfaction. She wore a yellow sweater and brown slacks that matched her gold-flecked chestnut hair, and he saw that her breasts were delightful, firm and full, but not heavy, not shaped by a brassiere; these beautiful breasts she kept hidden under that coat. With a little motion of her hand, as if they were now in some large rich foyer and not in a little hall, she said, "Now you're here you might as well come in and sit down."

At one time the living room must have been small, but the wall between it and what had been a dining room had been knocked out, and as he looked around he could hardly hide his astonishment. It was plain now why there was a need for a little extra money, unless her father was rich or was in a very well-paid profession. On the length of the floor there was a rich blue Chinese rug with a centre yellow pattern, the pattern repeated at the corners. The table lights must have been made from antique vases. The window drapes were of heavy gold brocade, and the wood of the little tables and high-backed chairs was old, and polished to bring out its natural warmth. "Nice place you have here, Ilona," he said, sitting down.

"We like it," she said, and then, her head on one side, "but Mr. Dubuque . . ."

"Yeah?"

"I don't think I need you."

"Could I take off my coat?" She took his coat, went into a cupboard in the hall, and returned.

"And now?" she asked, standing in front of him, her arms folded.

"Ilona," he began, "you know Frankie Spagnola?"

"Oh, Frankie Spagnola."

"He has his ladies."

"I said to him, go away, dirt."

"So he takes his time. Did he threaten you last night, or today?"

"Keep your voice down," and she looked at the staircase. "Please."

"I'm a businessman," he said more calmly. "I have to have an eye for the impression people make. I deal with conventions from all over the world. Sit down, please, let me finish." When she faced him in a carved and high-backed old chair, he went on. "Like I say, Ilona, you have a very special quality. A very unusual thing. Like a gift."

"A gift? I wonder," she repeated slowly, half to herself, as if he had touched something she believed in. "A gift."

"It surely is," he said. "Now look. It's my experience that people pay a lot of money to have very rare things. I hate to see rare, lovely things going cheap. When a lovely thing is so cheap that anybody can pick it up, then all lovely things are degraded. Right? It's degradation, Ilona, real degradation." Leaving the lounge to go his way, she would still be whoring, but as his voice took on an eager, insistent conviction, her face changed, her eyes softened, her mouth opened a little in a dreamy satisfaction she got from recognizing the remarkable value he placed on her as a person. He thought he could feel her coming a little closer.

Keeping his voice down, aware that her mother might be listening, he said, "You need money, Ilona. Okay. The money will be there. I'll see to it myself. Oh, I'll get it back. People are going to pay just to have you around, just because you are so uniquely what you are." Though she couldn't help being flattered at the way he was enlarging her as a person, he honestly didn't believe he was enlarging her. "Let me go on," he said. "The thing is to get you known. Ilona Tomory! Who is Ilona? That fabulous girl up there with something all men reach for. Who is she? The name is great. Ilona Tomory. Oh, I like it. Now, with your approval, this is the thing I have in mind."

And he told her that he knew just the right place, Muldoon's, the place on Jarvis with some real class, in sound financial condition, a first-class restaurant and lounge with a lively trade, college groups, young professional men . . . an expensive place. Free-wheeling, too. The manager, Tom Muldoon, owed him a few favors. Financial matters. Bad debts collected. Well, Muldoon liked to create an intimate club atmosphere for his drinking crowd. "The thing is to get you introduced, just introduced. You could be sitting at a table in the audience. Not on the stage. You have no training. But the guy says, 'In the audience tonight is the Hungarian personality Ilona Tomory.' It's done all the time, and you merely stand up. I hear the applause. Then, 'I wonder if

Miss Tomory would come up here.' Elegant, aloof, absolutely high-class. Then he coaxes you to do something, a little thing, nothing like the sophisticated dancer they've got there. A snatch of a song in half a minute. Just like saying hello, then laughing you run back to your table, with everybody saying, 'Who the hell is this lovely Ilona Tomory?'"

"Mr. Dubuque, for God's sake, no."

"Why?"

"I can't even carry a tune."

There was a descending footstep on the stairs, and as he stood up apprehensively, a tall woman came into the room, the pulled-back grey hair accentuating the face's clean, fine lines and long neck, like Ilona's. She was in a Chinese lounging-pyjama suit of beautiful shimmering blue silk, richly embroidered, which looked as if it might have been in a trunk for hundreds of years.

"Mother, Mr. Dubuque," Ilona said, and as she and her mother exchanged smiles, the mother put out her hand, holding it a little high as if she expected him to kiss it, though he had never kissed a woman's hand. "Ah, Mr. Dubuque, a friend of Ilona's, no?"

"I admire Ilona," he said. "I came to talk business. We've been talking business." The mother and Ilona had such ease with each other and with him that he grew flustered. The ease told him at once that Ilona, in not coming to his office, was confident she could compel him to come to her house. She might even have been expecting him. And this mother, in that gorgeous suit, could she have been tipped off that he would come? Or did she wear the outfit loafing around the house? How could he be sure? "I hope I didn't disturb you, barging into your house like this, Mrs. Tomory," he said. "I understand you've been ill."

"You were right to come," she said. "Now let us all sit down. There now." Each of her words was clear, yet she had Ilona's attractive accent. "Well, go on with your talk. I'll do what I intended to do," she said, and, getting up, went out to the hall and returned with the long mink coat. Sitting down again, she took from her pyjama pocket a tiny cushion full of needles; one of the needles was already threaded, and she opened the coat, so that the lining fell on her knees. "There's a bit of lining here I wanted to fix if I'm to go out tomorrow," she said. "Well, now, Jay Dubuque. A friend of Ilona's," she said, smoothing the coat lining with her hands. Her beautiful light-blue eyes seemed too bright in the pale face. "You were talking about the theatre, weren't you?"

"We were. If I disturbed you, Mrs. Tomory, I apologize," he said.

"I don't know that I'm really ill," she said. "Just a little run-down."

"What does the doctor say?" he asked politely.

"I'll see him again tomorrow. It was ridiculous. I was downtown. Coming home out there on the street near the corner I got weak. I could hardly move. I'm ashamed to say I had to sit down on the curb and rest. And one of my neighbors—I've always been courteous to Mrs. Dobbs, haven't I, Ilona?—I heard her say, 'If she can wear that kind of a coat, you'd think she'd be riding in a taxi.' Well, they had to help me home. And of course doctors nowadays can't make house calls. . . ."

"I know one who will, Mrs. Tomory," he said, trying to assert himself.

"I don't think our doctor liked the way Ilona talked to him on the phone. Oh, dear. I can remember when a doctor's visit was a pleasant social occasion. We would have some wine and biscuits and good conversation and feel we were important human beings. But never mind me. Are you in the theatre, Mr. Dubuque?"

"I'm what they call, I think, an entrepreneur."

"An entrepreneur? Well, in our home in Budapest—Ilona wouldn't remember, she was a little child—we used to hear such good talk about the theatre. And not so long ago, even in this city. Remember, Ilona, how your father and I would come in with friends after seeing a play? Now I never hear a young man of yours talking about the theatre. Why is that, Ilona?"

"It's my fault, I'm sure," said Ilona, shrugging it off with a little laugh. Then, jesting with her mother, "Or maybe such gentlemen I'm with, after a little talk with me, say to themselves, 'The theatre. Oh, she'd have such strong opinions. Wait till another time.' Or maybe I go to the wrong places."

The wrong places? The lounge of the Bradley. The exchange of smiles was a little too knowing, after the jesting, like a slip in a performance. No one was more wary of being conned than Jay. He told himself, The mother must know that Ilona is a whore, so they must be giving me an extension of the gentle-dignity routine Ilona used in the Bradley. But why were they working this on him?

"Yes, we always are what we are," the mother said. "You are what you are, Ilona," she said with real pride, and an astonishing fine approving smile.

"Yes. To be what you are," Jay said. "That's the thing."

"Ilona reads to me, you know, Mr. Dubuque. It's lovely for me because she can always tell the mood I'm in. She's sensitive. She can make my mood beautiful by reading me the right poem. I actually manage to feel beautiful."

"Well, you can't beat that," Jay said.

"Mother," Ilona said, keeping a straight face, "Mr. Dubuque would like me to sing for him."

"He would?" she asked, smiling. "No, Ilona hasn't a voice, Mr. Dubuque. Robert knew she didn't have a voice. He tried to get her to sing."

"Robert?"

"She was engaged to Robert. He's away now, in Hungary."

"I see."

"And Robert knew she couldn't sing."

"Maybe she can't sing, but she's got a special kind of low voice," Jay said stubbornly. "One of those foggy voices that gets to a man."

"But not a singing voice, Mr. Dubuque."

"So what?" He got up, and, walking up and down, concentrated, then suddenly turned, beaming. "I've got it," he said.

"You've got what, Mr. Dubuque?"

"Repertoire. All that's needed is half a minute. A taste. A sample of the goods. What do those stars who can't sing worth a damn do? Just talk it to a beat, back-up music like you read the poems to your mother, only this is to music, for thirty seconds." Carried away as he was and pacing up and down, he didn't care that they were shaking their heads. A big, slow grin on his face, he stood still. "I've got it. By God, I've got it. And it's foolproof. It's European. It's old. And in Ilona's foggy talking voice, wonderful."

"For God's sake, what's wonderful?" Ilona said.

"Mack the Knife."

"Yeah, you know, Mack the Knife."

"I know Mack the Knife."

"Something like this," and he started clapping his

hands to the rhythmic beat, trying to say huskily, " 'Oh, the shark has . . . pearly teeth, dear . . . and he keeps them . . . shining bright . . .' Oh, boy, that in your foggy voice, Ilona. Come on, try it with me. 'La-de da da . . . la-de da da . . . and he keeps them . . . da-da-da.' Then, you walk off."

His sense of conviction was so compelling she stopped laughing and looked at her mother. "Hell, it's just like you reading a poem, only with your body you slink a little. Keep saying it. See, it'll go on in your head all night. Ah, you're great, kid, isn't she, Mrs. Tomory?"

"Go get the guitar, Ilona," Mrs. Tomory said.

When Ilona returned with the guitar, her mother, putting it on her knee and smiling, said, "I'll just chord for you, Ilona. Why not?" She began to chord, and Ilona, her forearm on the back of a tall antique chair, sang, "Oh, the shark has . . . pearly teeth, dear . . ." swaying her body.

"Not bad, Ilona darling," her mother said.

"The thing is," Jay said, waving his hands around in excitement, "you're to be there so briefly, just a snatch. A taste. Just a sample . . . gracious-like, and they all wish you were still there."

But then, hearing the front door open, he turned. Someone in the hall was removing rubbers and a slicker, then a man in his late fifties came in wearing an official cap and matching windbreaker and carrying a flashlight. A man from the gas company just walking in? Startled, Jay turned to Ilona. "This is Jay Dubuque, Father," she said to this man, and then to Jay, with pride and a noble air of giving him a privilege, "My father," she said, and took her father's arm.

"Mr. Dubuque," said the man from the gas company. After appraising Jay calmly, and nodding with princely approval, he put out his hand, the flashlight still in his other hand, but with such an air of distinction that Jay himself wanted to appear at his best.

"Excuse me, Mr. Dubuque," the father said, turning to his wife. "No. Terezia, please . . ." he said, drawing her up from the chair. "Back to bed. You told me you wouldn't get up today. It was to be tomorrow perhaps." He, too, had splendid, slightly accented diction. They all spoke beautifully, but with the same little foreign rhythm. "Don't worry about me, Terezia," he said. "Ilona can get me something to eat."

"Well, good night, Mr. Dubuque, and you, my darling," the mother said.

"Good night, Mrs. Tomory."

"You'll come again?"

"I'll come again."

"And so, we'll meet again. How nice," and they heard her going up the stairs.

"Well now, Mr. Dubuque," Mr. Tomory said, putting down his cap and his flashlight. His grey hair was smoothed back and he had a small grey moustache. "If my wife enjoyed talking to you, I'm sure I will, too."

"Oh, no, I won't stay."

"Do stay, sir. I always like a little rest before eating. It's a regrettable fact that my feet get tired. What business are you in, Mr. Dubuque?"

"Conventions. Mortgages. Consumer services. I've told Ilona she would be good on the stage. She has a real presence. I see you have a position with the gas company."

"I read gas meters, Mr. Dubuque."

"Well . . . at least you get around."

"Indeed I do, sir. A man to whom no door is shut." While her father laughed so indulgently, Jay noticed that

Ilona joined in his good humor with warm, affectionate approval. "As a philosopher, and I've become a philosopher," her father went on, "I know my work has incredible advantages. Great freedom of movement, great freedom of thought, and exercise that stimulates this mental activity."

"A job that gives a man a chance to be himself," Jay said awkwardly. "I don't know. As your wife says, you all like to be yourselves. Well, who doesn't?"

"The Tomorys, yes," he agreed. "We're that kind of a family. I think we do it very well, no?"

"You sure do," Jay said, glancing at Ilona, who nodded gravely.

"Father, don't you think I should be getting your dinner?" she asked.

"Yes, and I do have to go," Jay said.

"All in good time. Don't hurry, Mr. Dubuque. I'm relaxing," and he stretched back in his chair. "All day long I go without finding anyone to talk to. I go into dark cellars. I'm a man who follows the beam of a flashlight into the cellars of the world," and he chuckled, pleased with himself. "You see," he said, waving his hand at the furniture, "I used to be in the antique business. From the time we came here." Very much at ease with himself, he went on, "I made some bad investments. Got heavily in debt. Oh, the antique business! Suddenly all that is junk becomes antique. Junk became very expensive. Everybody has some junk. Every piece of junk from every old barn in Quebec was suddenly expensive. That and my debts. We went bankrupt, Mr. Dubuque," and then, after pondering, he went on, "It's a peculiar world we live in now. Not like Budapest used to be. This town is full of money, yet thousands are out of work. I kept losing jobs. Maybe the Tomorys weren't born to work for other people. Ah, but I hit on it. Oh, I did," and he came leaning forward brightly. "Mr. Dubuque, what is it that every house needs in good or bad times, at all times?"

"Well, let me see. . . ."

"Cooking, heating, especially in this wintry country. Gas, Mr. Dubuque. Am I right?"

"Right."

"And someone has to read the gas meters. They're always there, the meters. That's security. Well, now I've got security, Mr. Dubuque," and as he leaned back at ease, Ilona nodded approvingly.

"Yes, it's worked out so well for us," she said, sharing the ease, her eyes showing she was proud of him, as they were all proud of each other. But why? Dubuque couldn't make up his mind, feeling as he did that he had been watching in slow motion a movie going on in another city, the people moving around with a strange formal grace while watching and listening intently, and he was trying to figure out what they were doing and why it was so important to know.

"I'm holding you up, Mr. Tomory," he said with sudden appreciative good humor. "Anyway, I have to go. I'm glad I met you," and he shook hands with as courtly an air as he could manage. In the hall, when Ilona was giving him his coat, he chuckled. "You're wonderful, and your father and mother are wonderful. We'll have lunch tomorrow. Right?"

"If you'd like."

"I'll call you at twelve-thirty. Later tonight I'm going in to see my friend Muldoon. I have the right feeling about this thing, Ilona. A hunch," and he couldn't hide his elation.

"And I have, too," she said softly, as if they had a secret understanding.

His eyes were on her breasts and she knew it, knew her breasts made him happy. The light overhead was in a marble globe like a gold moon and she was standing beside the vase of yellow roses. The gold moon and the yellow roses, and she had heard herself called "Countess Cunt", and knew he had heard it, too, yet she smiled as if he must know that nothing had been, or could be, taken from her.

"Mr. Dubuque . . ." she said.

"Jay. . . ."

"Jay, I don't know what you really think, but I know you really value me."

"What did I do, Ilona? What did I say?"

"I told you I didn't like your smile, remember. It cheapened things."

"Yeah, I remember."

"Well, not now. I like it now."

"Really. How so?"

"I don't know. There was a glint in it. Pleasure, and a real glint."

"We're on our way," he said, and they shook hands decorously. But outside, smiling to himself, he turned and looked back at the house. Not a light to be seen. Drapes were drawn on all the windows. It had begun to snow again and the falling snow made the commonplace, cheap little house just a heavy shadow between the two other lighted, snow-covered little houses. Then he had a feeling that was strange to him; a feeling that in there, in the shadows, was an antique theatre with antique furniture and rugs, and the figures in there that had moved around so gracefully were still going on with their pretending. And yet, he thought, they couldn't really believe in any of it, any more than he could believe in them, as figures or persons—or could he? Ilona knew she was a whore, and her father was only a little guy with a flashlight, and her mother was only playing the duchess in some great Chinese lady's ancient pyjamas, and yet he could get the hang of why they were doing it. They knew what had happened to them and what they were now, but each one was proud of the other's performance as figures of dignity and respect.

12

NEXT DAY IN THE COURTYARD CAFÉ, FREQUENTED BY television people, gossip columnists, and men on the fringe of movie-making, all looking their best, everyone was aware of anyone who came in, and they couldn't help noticing Ilona with her superior air and her long mink coat. In no time, Sherman Schatzky, so close-shaven, so shining pink he could have been lifted out of a vat of boiling water and placed in his pale-grey checked suit, came to their table. Schatzky, who raised money for low-budget movies, had an excuse to speak to Dubuque. His Montreal uncle had used Jay to put some heavy pressure on a man who owed him money. From what he had heard, Schatzky was afraid of Dubuque. Now he asked him if he had seen his uncle recently. Schatzky's shrewd, probing, money-making eyes were met squarely by Ilona's, with all her Bradley-lounge wisdom. It put Schatzky off a little.

"Lovely sunlight today, Miss Tomory," he said.

"The snow melts. It melts too quickly," she said.

"You really like the winter?"

"Snow is lovely when the weather is mild," she said, with just a trace of an accent. No longer sure of himself, Schatzky returned to his table.

"Don't look that way, Ilona," Jay said. "The first thing he says sitting down is, 'Who is Ilona Tomory?' You can bet on it."

" 'Who is Ilona Tomory?' " she repeated thoughtfully. "I like that. I like it very much." He had slipped the coat off her shoulders, draping it around the back of the chair, saying, "I like that dress." It was a light-blue dress, high at the throat and with a dark-blue strip three inches wide running from the neck to the hem, and on the shoulders and down the front there was a pattern like a dark-blue scroll on the light-blue. "Where did you get the dress?" he asked.

"In a little shop in Yorkville," she said. "It's a Scandinavian dress; a girl in the shop lets me know when something I like comes in and puts it aside." She was studying the menu, frowning. Finally she said, "I'll have smoked salmon and very thin slices of pumpernickel. And some white wine."

"I don't know much about you, Ilona," he said, when they were eating.

As he expected, she said, "Nor I about you. Just where do you come from?"

"Me? I used to be a magician. I had a hobby. An illusionist."

"Were you any good?"

"Not nearly as good as you."

"You puzzle me," she said, frowning. Yet she showed no further curiosity about him, as if he were just a money man, and it hurt; he wanted to talk, to open up hidden corners in the city's life for her, and his own big corner. Then she smiled, not at him, but at a black-haired, blue-eyed girl about to leave a balding, grey-suited man of forty who held on to her hand. The man, stroking the hand, took it in both of his and kissed it, and the girl, bending quickly, kissed the hands folded over hers. And then, her eyes meeting Ilona's, she, too, smiled and Dubuque said, "Yeah. Well, look, I know there had to be a guy somewhere in your life. Who's this Robert you were engaged to? Who's Robert?"

"My mother told you about Robert."

"You tell me about Robert."

"What do you care?"

"It's something more to know about you."

"I'm here. We're getting along. No?"

"I say to myself, Ilona. Who is Ilona?"

"I'm Ilona."

"Come on, Ilona. When's Robert coming back?"

"Well, some say he died in Hungary."

"You don't think so?"

"You're okay, Mr. Dubuque. Only I don't think you'd understand."

"I'm no dummy. Look, we're a team now. I should know some things. For instance, what do I do if this Robert shows up and you're working with me?"

"What would I do? Dear God, what would I do?" she said, half to herself, her eyes shifting away to the sunken floor alongside the row of tables. On this sunken floor stood a long dessert table on which were laid out cakes and pastries and creams. "Isn't that a Black Forest cake there?" she asked, leaning over. "I love it. If you get me a piece, maybe I'll tell you about Robert."

"It's a deal," he said.

When he was getting the cake, she sat lost in

thought, her elbows on the table, her hands clasped under her chin in sunlight coming from the roof. This café had little interest for Dubuque, yet it had an attractive feature. When the sun shone, with all the greenery around and with the glass ceiling high above, the naked girders and tables were bathed in light; yet in the sudden golden light, Ilona, off by herself, did not look quite right for the place.

"Oh, doesn't it look good?" she said when he returned to the table and the cake was put before her. "Oh, it is good. Do you want a little piece?" While she ate slowly and with relish, he watched her lips and her tongue, the tip of her tongue, till she leaned back, her napkin at her lips. "Well, Robert, eh?" she said. "It's a fact they wanted me to marry Robert." Then she went on in an even tone to tell him about Robert, pausing sometimes to smile and say, "And then . . ." and moments later, "And so then . . . ," making it sound like a story, or maybe because it had become a story for her.

Robert, who had lived with his uncle's family in Austria since he was five years old, had come here three years ago to live with his aunt Marika, she said. His father and mother had been killed in the revolt of '56. This aunt Marika had made a successful career for herself in real estate. Quite a woman, Marika! In Budapest she had been an interior decorator, and a friend of Cardinal Mindszenty. "My mother, who knew her in the good old days in Budapest," Ilona said, "was amused by her airs." But Marika had done well here, had got bank loans and bought up fine old houses in Rosedale, decorated them, and resold them at great profit, and now she had one of them herself, all redone behind a high brown stained fence and with strange expensive trees with drooping branches on the lawn. Though she did her business in

English, Marika had made her own house a little Hungary, where the style, the food, the friends, and the talk were from the days in Budapest. A thin, tall, proud woman, she kept a huge Irish wolfhound named Rolf. "My own parents had got tired of going to Marika's," Ilona said. "You wouldn't know this, Mr. Dubuque, but all kinds of Hungarians got into this country after that revolt. Crooks, criminals, good people. The best fighters had all been killed in the revolt, or afterwards. Hungarians here are a broken-up community. . . . Understand?"

"Not all aristocrats?" he said grinning.

"You're damn right," she said solemnly. Then she explained that the same people had been going to Marika's place for years, always the same ones, still believing they were in touch with friends in Hungary, a network planning another great revolt against this, what do you call it, regime. That was it. The godless regime. And they read their letters from home to each other, were very devout and prayed together, and her father often joked about Marika and her friends acting as if they were a government in exile. Marika, she was sure, was glad when her father's business failed and he had to take the job with the gas company. Well, Robert came to live with Marika, who set him up in a Hungarian bookstore, a store dealing in books and memorabilia about the old Hungary.

"I remember the day I dropped in to the store," she said. Robert wouldn't talk to her in English, she went on, though he could speak the language, and her own Hungarian wasn't good, and because she had grown up here he treated her like an alien. He had fair hair, fine features, and good shoulders, and a head full of dreams about a Hungary he had never really seen, stuff drilled into him in Austria, and he was contemptuous of everything around him here. He was a prince in exile who knew he didn't belong here, waiting to be called home, all tightened up while he waited, nervous, expectant, his hands held straight at his sides. He had no friends his own age, just that old crowd, the old ones at Marika's place with their funny clothes, the old ones, all adoring him. She found out that he wouldn't even read the local newspapers, knew nothing about the city and didn't care to, since he was certain his real life was to be somewhere else. Well, she felt sorry for him. When Marika was having one of her Hungarian evenings, she would invite Ilona to be company for Robert. "And then . . ." she began, hesitating, smiling slowly to herself, her eyes lowered, "Well, why not?" she said, and went on with the story.

After one of her dinners, Marika and her friends went on to the opera, leaving her alone with Robert, who was stretched out on the couch ten feet away, listening to some classical records, record after record, for what was there to talk about? They couldn't have a conversation. Lying there, he looked so lonely, so out of place, so far away from any kind of a home, and any life for himself aside from the dreams in his head, that her heart melted. They had no words, no thoughts they could share. Getting up, and stepping across the big wolfhound asleep on the rug, she knelt by the dog, and said gently, "Robert. Come on. Come on." Holding his lonely eyes with hers, she undid her blouse, baring her breasts, and took his hand and put it on her breast. "Then, well then," Ilona said, "I took him into the bedroom and fucked him."

"Good for you," Dubuque said.

"Thanks," she said. But the trouble was, Robert was very devout, as were Marika and her friends, for the church gave strength to their tradition. He took her to church, had her pray with him, then asked her to promise to marry him. "Robert, look," she said, laughing, "you don't have to marry me. I don't want to get married." But he took it for granted they would marry. And Marika, who would have approved of the marriage, told everyone they were engaged. Even her own father and mother talked about the engagement. Finally, she herself went to Marika and said, "What is this? You might as well know I'm not getting married. I've told Robert I couldn't marry him." Later, Marika, coming home early one night, found them in bed. "Whore . . . a born whore," she said.

After an angry quarrel with Marika, Robert left her place and took a small apartment near his bookstore. He kept coming after Ilona and sleeping with her, which was so moving because bit by bit she could see a beautiful change coming over his life, all from a few nights of loving her. That she could do this for him filled her with wonder. It was like the discovery of something secret and good in her; it began to fascinate her. How could she bear to tell him now to go back to being a lonely, out-of-place exile? "I may have had an effect on Robert, Mr. Dubuque," she said. "But maybe he had an effect on me, too, or maybe I wouldn't be here with you now. I don't know." She shrugged.

Anyway, she went on, Robert must have told himself, or Marika maybe suggested to him, that she couldn't belong only to him; he was too out of place in her world. So, putting all talk of Hungary aside, he began to talk only in English and to read the newspaper carefully, talking always about what was going on, one night insisting they go to the ball park though she didn't care for baseball, and one night they went to the Bradley House bar, and one other night when she was whistling that catchy tune "Sweet Georgia Brown" he whistled with her, and got up and danced. Things like that were going on all the time.

They tried new restaurants, and he even tried smoking a little pot, though she told him she didn't need pot or any other drug. In his bookstore he got in contemporary Hungarian journals and soon had new customers coming in, and he also wanted to meet her girl friends, the friends she'd made working as a receptionist downtown. The three girls from the office with whom she lunched and had drinks at Maloney's bar after work all liked Robert for his elegant manners and joked about her having a fling with him. They called her a loner, "Ilona, the loner".

As for Marika, her fiery Hungarian temperament now bored Robert. That old crowd were ghosts, he said. Times change, he said. As they all got grey hair, their clothes looked funnier. Marika was aware of the change in him. On one of those special evenings, Marika, coming up behind her with a falsely warm, comforting smile, whispered, "I think I know why you won't marry Robert, my dear. You're wondering if you don't have a whore's temperament and Robert is too good for you. But how do you know?" The gentle whisper made the viciousness all the worse. "Oh, la-di-da," she said, laughing at Marika.

Yet that night she caught Robert watching her with a melancholy expression. After they had gone to bed, he said, "Marika will say anything these days, won't she? Why is she so mad at you? Why does she say you have a whore's temperament? What does it mean, Ilona?"

Eying Dubuque, she seemed to be waiting for some shrewd worldly comment. When he said nothing, she shrugged. "Okay, the fact is I didn't know anything about whores. I had taken a secretarial course. I was a receptionist at a small advertising agency. I had never met a whore, and wouldn't have known where to go to meet one, and had never even wondered what they were like. When I laughed at Robert, it was a way of laughing at all the dead things Marika stood for, I think. Yes, I think so. Yes, I'm sure of it."

"Just the same," and she hesitated. "Oh, I don't know." She couldn't say what was in Robert's head at the time. His mood had changed. He grew very gentle. Rubbing his fingers through her hair, he told her he would never forget how lovely it had been the first night she took him to bed. Yet why had she done it? Why? She told him it was because he had looked so lonely and out of place. Thinking this over, he teased her.

"What about all the other lonely men around here? I'd better look out."

She gave him a thump in the ribs with her elbow and got up to get dressed. "What time is it?" she said.

"Ten after ten."

"I said I'd be home."

When he was helping her pull her dress over her head and shoulders, he asked, "Why aren't you sure? Please tell me, Ilona, why not just me?"

She told him she was convinced he knew in his heart he did not really belong here with her, for just last night she had heard him dreaming of that crazy undiscovered Hungary of his. All he was doing was trying to make himself feel at home here, just to be happy with her. "Am I really wrong?" she asked.

It astonished him that she had been able to see that he had been thinking so much about Hungary. It was Marika's doing, keeping after him about Hungary. Marika was suffering, and she was right to bring her suffering to him, since he owed her so much.

Until that night, Ilona hadn't known about Marika's brother and the two grown sons in Hungary to whom she sent money. They corresponded with her regularly, giving her guarded news, and Marika thought of them as part of her network; sometimes their letters were in a code. But for months now she hadn't heard from them. Her roundabout inquiries had led her nowhere. The family had vanished. Convinced they had been executed, or were in prison, she had been asking friends to pray for them. "What you should do, Ilona," Robert said, "is come with me and help me console Marika. I owe it to her." And the next night they went to console Marika.

It became a very emotional evening. Having Robert there consoling her made Marika weep. Carried away by all the weeping, Robert suggested he should go to Budapest. People were going back and forth now. The regime in Budapest? How could they have anything against him? Marika wouldn't hear of it at first. "No, no. Absolutely no," she said. But as she circled around, making fierce, firm gestures, the idea began to excite her, and with tears in her eyes she threw her arms around Robert, her own dear boy again. "Yes," she said. "Yes!" When Robert asked, "What do you think, Ilona?" she agreed. Why shouldn't he go, if he felt he had to? She knew Robert would never be happy till he saw Hungary again.

The thing was settled. Marika was to provide the money. It took a week to make the preparations. Robert got many addresses from Marika and many instructions. Ilona went with him to the airport, and, kissing her, he held her a long time, saying little. He walked towards the entrance for passengers, then came back. "I kept thinking you'd say you wanted to come, Ilona," he said. "I waited to hear it." Then he was gone.

Two weeks later, she got a short letter from Robert in which he said she shouldn't worry, he was well, and was enjoying himself looking around, meeting people and liking what he saw, and pretending to himself she was with him. Marika also got a letter which upset her. Robert had located her brother and his family. They weren't in prison, they were in good health and cheerful. Then Ilona got another letter. Robert couldn't get her out of his mind. Would she come to him? He couldn't believe that in the end she wouldn't want to come. "Come. Come. And we can make a life together. Come. Come," he wrote.

She wrote an affectionate letter in which she said she had always felt good when with him, but he must have known he could never have all of her.

When they didn't hear again from Robert, Marika, convinced that he had been picked up by the police and imprisoned or executed, asked everyone to pray that he had not become another Christian martyr. "My mother kept telling me about Marika's distress . . . this poor woman, Marika." One night she decided she owed it to Robert, and to Marika too, to tell her that Robert was obviously doing what he wanted to do, staying in Hungary, and liking it.

At nine that evening she went around to his aunt's place. At the door, blocking the way, staring at her blankly, Marika looked like an outraged great lady in her long green scarf and with her hair piled high. Her face started twisting, her eyes blazed. "You . . . you come here!" she hissed in Hungarian.

"Marika," Ilona said, reaching out sympathetically. "It's about Robert. Things you should know about Robert. He's okay. It's like he went home. That's all."

"Home?" Marika cried, pulling away. It was plain now that she understood very well that Robert had ditched her, and her crowd. Her mouth was ugly. "You drove him to it," she said bitterly. "You, you whore," and she grabbed her arm. "To pleasure yourself you took him away from us. Robert learned you couldn't really belong to him or anyone. He couldn't face it, could he? You know he couldn't. You knew you couldn't belong to one man, not even Robert. You're a natural-born whore, God damn you; get out of here."

"Marika, you're crazy," she said. "A real crazy. Too crazy to see anything. Just remember this, Robert has a good memory of me." Then she couldn't get her breath.

"I said, go," Marika cried. "Don't stand there. Go. No? I'll fix you." She called out, "Rolf, Rolf," and when the big Irish wolfhound came trotting along the hall she made a hissing noise, pointing. "Sic her," she hissed. Responding obediently, the big dog came at Ilona. Scared, she ran down the path through the strange drooping trees, the dog growling at her heels. At the gate, she panicked. The gate was closed and she fumbled with the catch. Her body sagging, she fell to her knees, while the wolfhound, all silvered in the moonlight, its bared teeth shining, snapped at her, growling. When she held out her arms, shivering, down on her knees, the dog wavered, sniffing at her hands, remembering her. Then he wagged his tail, and with an awkward, almost apologetic, shake of his big body, he came brushing against her, licking at her face.

"Rolf," Marika cried, taking a few steps forward.

Then, stunned, she stopped, and sounding frightened called, "Rolf." She pleaded, "Rolf, Rolf, come back here, come back."

"Go on, boy. Go on," Ilona said, pointing to Marika. Then, opening the gate, her heart pounding wildly and sick with humiliation, she ran along the street, running till she could no longer get her breath. Going over the bridge that spans the ravine, she got out of the neighborhood. Since she couldn't bear to go home and talk to her parents, her sense of deepening shame became a rage. She was trembling. She had to sit down.

A church was just ahead, and she remembered she had once been in this church with Robert. He had known a Hungarian family living in the nearby huge apartment building. Ducking into the church, she sat down in a pew halfway down the aisle. Only three people were in the church, a young woman kneeling in the centre aisle, her head buried in her hands, and two sad beaten-up old men in a pew to the left. But when she closed her eyes, the raging protest began to well up in her again. One leg trembled. She pushed her foot hard against the floor. Then, unable to sit still, she left the pew, and, standing in the aisle facing the altar, she saw the many lighted candles over to the side, and an old woman lighting a candle.

Without thinking about what she was doing, she went slowly up the aisle, over to the candles, lit one, stared at the flickering flame, then took another one and lit it, too. As the flame of her two candles brightened, she seemed to hear Marika shrieking wildly, "Whore! Natural-born whore!" But the candle flames seemed to mock the cries, and then she could hear Robert telling her how good she had been for him and now, thanks to her, he could possess his own soul in peace—because she was as she was, because of what she could do for a man, because of a hidden wonder in her. And then her heart took a leap and she began to exult in what she was. Then, hearing again Marika yelling, "Goddamn natural-born whore," she exulted even more. And the flames of all the candles in the circle, brightening for her, went on mocking Marika.

13

AND NOW, IN THE CAFÉ, AFTER LOOKING AROUND with a faint smile she said to Dubuque, "Well, there you are. That's who Robert is."

"Is it all true, Ilona?"

"What?"

"Even the part about the dog?"

"Maybe I have a way with dogs . . . and men."

"It's a good story," he said dubiously. "Only . . ."

"Only what?"

"Only it doesn't sound right for you. That woman, Marika. No one lets someone else tell him what he is unless he really wants to believe it."

"Mr. Dubuque," she said with dignity, "I am what I am," and her eyes with their deep warmth, and the sadness behind the warmth, were as beautiful as any he had ever seen. "I know plain fucking can be ugly. But it can be magic too."

"With you, I'm sure," he said, grinning.

"Thanks," she said.

"Just the same there are things about you I don't understand," he said.

"That's good."

"Good? Why?"

"You can keep on wondering. No?"

"Thanks," he said, baffled.

But the thing was, oh, the main thing was, she really could put herself in any light. "Rough as that Marika was, you knew how to handle it, didn't you?" he said, confident beyond all doubt that if she were in the right mood, if she really wanted to do it, she could easily make a grand and regal impression at Muldoon's. "Ilona, I'm still not sure where you really come from," he said admiringly, "but you've got it. You've really got it."

"I'll have to think that one over," she said. "Well, it was a very nice lunch, thank you. Shall we go?"

14

HE COULD HAVE TAKEN THE TIME TO FIND OUT ABOUT
the Tomorys and their friends, but to do so would have
gone against his grain. Edmund J. Dubuque letting someone else tell him about a woman? Would it matter if
some other broad, who claimed to know all about her,
described her as a perfect bitch who liked telling stories?
What would it have to do with her essentials? As long as
she could create illusions for a man who paid her, did
anything else matter?

Now, as they got into his car near the Courtyard,
he said, "I'll take you home and drive slowly by the park
where I used to play when I was a kid, and see if it looks
better in this strong sunlight. It looked pretty bleak the
other night."

"When you were a kid?" she said. "I don't think
you ever were a kid."

But when they drove by the park, shining white in
the sunlit snow, he talked about the old Haven House

and Tom Muldoon. The new lounge was now called The Muldoon. He said that Muldoon himself should get to know her. Muldoon needed the company of a girl like her. "He has respect for me," he said, grinning. "I feel sorry for Muldoon, even though he's rich."

He explained that Muldoon's wife, a nervous, dark-haired, intense woman, a painter who wasn't sure she had any talent, had left him six months ago. She had a friend, a feminist, big in the women's movement, who convinced her she shouldn't be satisfied with her husband's hotel life. So Muldoon's wife told him that whether she lived in a hovel or not she had to find out if she could have a rich independent life of her own. This had astonished poor Muldoon, who told her, "I'll be here, I don't care what you think. You'll come back and I'll be here waiting."

After six months, Muldoon's faith in his wife's return was just as strong as in the beginning, Dubuque said. Yet a man had no right to be such a fool, he said, especially when he had a lively, successful place like The Muldoon. Didn't she think so? he asked. No, she didn't. Muldoon sounded like her kind of man, and she hoped he would soon be asking who she was. He hoped so, too, he said. Some real money would be there for her with Muldoon. By this time they had come to her house. He would call for her at ten, he said, and went on his way to Muldoon's hotel.

It had been a sedate five-storeyed residential establishment, the sort of place where literary clubs held luncheons and where many of the comfortably well-off guests had settled in for years. But Muldoon, with his new lounge, had given the house another character. People from all over town now came to his dining room to enjoy the fine steaks, the expensive informality, the entertainment from one high-class performer, and the jolly sense of an affluent family conviviality. But at this hour in the afternoon the oak tables were deserted, the wrought-iron lights on the walls dimmed. The oak-panelled walls seemed to belong to a deserted baronial hall, the gleam and shine were still on the long polished oak bar and on the heavy overhanging ceiling beams. Only one patron sat at the bar. "I'll have my brandy, Joe," Dubuque said to the barman.

"Right, Mr. Dubuque."

"Is Tom Muldoon around?"

"He should be in shortly, sir."

"Tell him I'd like a word."

"As soon as he comes in, Mr. Dubuque," Joe said respectfully.

Turning on his stool, Dubuque surveyed the lounge which he was sure was just the right place for Ilona. There it was—the little stage. As he stared at it the room came alive for him: all the regulars there; the people at the oaken tables, and the lights coming on after Chita; and then at the tables the talk about Chita's startlingly explicit sexual dance; then a burst of laughter, followed by a few quiet minutes; and at last there she was on the stage, and people were asking, "Who is this Ilona Tomory?"

The big dark-haired fellow in the conservative blue suit four stools away was drunk enough to be over-whelmingly convivial. He said to Dubuque, "We've met, haven't we?"

"What?"

"We met somewhere and talked. Where was it?"

"You don't know me," Jay said.

"More's the pity."

"So it is," Jay said, turning away. The young man,

who was in the bar night and day, and lived in an apartment just a block up the street, was Johnny Sills. He was the son of Rupert Sills of the uranium mines, a man with too much money and a big mouth. Johnny Sills came here in the afternoons as well as the evenings, as if it were the only place where he felt at home.

"Can I buy you a drink, sir?" Sills asked.

"I have a drink."

"Well, so have I. Oh, I intrude, I see." In this young man's face was some sweetness mixed up with a slumbering aggressiveness. He didn't look like his father. This had been noted recently by regulars at the bar when father and son had their pictures in the paper. They had both made the news. The pictures had been taken in the great house ten miles beyond the city where old Sills kept eighteen antique cars. The picture of the father was in the papers after he and a broker friend had exchanged wives. Rupert Sills and his pretty second wife and a stockbroker friend, Marlowe, who also had a pretty second wife, had gone to Mexico with these wives, got divorced, and then made the exchange.

And then three months later young Sills got his picture in the paper. He had gone berserk at the graduate school where he had been taking a Ph.D. in Near Eastern Studies. His expulsion had enraged his father, who never read books but wanted to have a professor in the family, just as he wanted to be a university governor himself. Young Sills, travelling in the East for three years, had got too interested in some Eastern religions. Under the gruelling pressure of preparation for his Ph.D. oral examination, he had cracked up. Facing his board of examiners, his mind whirled and turned on him. After letting out a wild shout, then a surprising string of obscenities, he had grabbed the chairs, one by one, and hurled them at the windows. The terrified professors called the police. His humiliated father paid for the damage. Now Johnny Sills, living up the street from Muldoon's, talked himself out every day at the bar.

"I'm sure I know you," he said, breaking in again on Jay's reverie.

"Sorry," Jay said abruptly. He called to the bartender, "Any sign of Tom Muldoon yet?"

"I think he just came in," the bartender said.

"Good," Jay said.

Moving three stools closer, Sills loomed up over Dubuque, a big powerful presence in a suit fitting him admirably when he was standing, but too tight when he sat; his thighs flattened and spread on the stool as he sat down. Dubuque looked at the suit, the three-piece dark, expensive suit, and grinned. What was going on in this town, he wondered. Now even drunken professors wore these executive three-piece business suits. Beneath his black hair Sills's face was flushed and restless. In the evenings his face was full of aggressive mockery, but now it had an expression of sweet friendliness, free of the drunken, lonely torment.

"Do you mind?" Sills asked.

"Do I mind what?"

"I say we talked before."

"I say I don't think so."

"I know who you are."

"Who am I?"

"You're The Man."

"Look, buster, I've things on my mind."

"The Man, I imagine, always has things on his mind."

"Yeah. And how would you like to take a walk?"

"Walk? Where to?"

"I said take a walk, buster."

"Take a walk. Yeah, that's interesting," and he nodded solemnly. "I've said it to myself many times. Do you know I've walked all over Europe?"

Dubuque couldn't be sure how drunk Sills was, so, half turning his back on him, he caught the bartender's eye and shrugged.

"I walked through the hill towns of northern Italy," Johnny Sills went on, "and then—it was in Orvieto, I think that's right. Not Assisi, Orvieto—and I had a long talk with an old philosopher. I got him to talk. We talked and talked till, being old, he got tired and sat down. Then he told me he had got the hang of me. I was walking the wrong way, he said, looking for things ahead out there, always ahead out there—journeying in the wrong direction. Now I should turn around, he said. I should look inward—go miles and miles inward through the jungle of the mind and heart. And if I kept on I would come to a clearing and see a new shiny image of myself. I think I see it, too. Yes, I think I do."

"So you do," Dubuque said, pointing to the bar mirror. "Right there in the mirror. See? And you look drunk to me. Well, I'm taking a walk now, too. Right into the washroom." But Muldoon, who had appeared at the other end of the bar, was beckoning. A big, handsome, quiet man with a black beard and the lonely light of faraway places in his eyes, he greeted Dubuque with respect.

Muldoon had to have respect for Dubuque, whom he shouldn't have known at all. The Muldoons were of an old monied family. The one in the family they all looked up to, even Muldoon himself, was Senator Muldoon, the white-bearded, florid-faced cake-and-biscuit manufacturer, who sat on hospital boards and headed charity drives and was a friend of the cardinal. The senator, an amateur gambler, had heard about Willie Connelly's hotel on the outskirts where there was a wheel and a big game. Some friends took him there after a Saturday-night party. At the end of the evening he owed the establishment $55,000; he paid by cheque. He knew he had been set up and cheated. When Tom Muldoon at the hotel heard about it, he was humiliated and outraged. He knew the venerated senator could not face the disgrace that would come if he laid a charge. What was to be done? Someone told Muldoon to see Dubuque. Dubuque was invited to the hotel. Three days later the $55,000 cheque was returned to the senator. Muldoon, a little awed by Dubuque, never asked what had happened, or who had got hurt. He said simply, "I owe you one, Dubuque. Feel at home in my place."

Dubuque said to him, "The spoiled rich kid has been bending my ear. Is he part of the furniture now?"

"Now, don't get Johnny wrong," Muldoon said. "He's all right. I've talked to him when he's sober. How would you like to have been pushed around by that old tyrant of a father, Rupert Sills? Ever meet him? Well, I have. All Johnny has been trying to do is divest himself of a thousand of those unwanted things. Well, what's on your mind, Dubuque?"

"A little favor. That's all. It's nothing," Dubuque said, noting the flicker of apprehension coming in Muldoon's eyes. He told him he had a talented girl who looked like a princess and was soon going to be well known, and he merely wanted to have her introduced while she sat at his table tonight. It was the kind of thing so often done in this lounge, and it should happen right after the sexy Chita had finished her number and gone back to her hotel, and then Jimmie Sykes could ask Ilona to step up on the stage, have her talk-sing a few bars of "Mack the Knife", and laugh, wave, and hurry back to her table, all taking about two minutes. "The kind of thing that's often done around here, eh?" he said. "You like to have it often, don't you?" And Muldoon, delighted to find this first repayment favor was so small, said, "Fine, fine. I'll speak to Jimmie Sykes. These things make everybody feel we're having a party, don't they?"

"And if you're around, you'll be the first one asking me to introduce you to her, and I will," Dubuque said. He reserved the table for ten-thirty that evening. They shook hands as if they really liked each other.

Outside, the street lights were coming on and down the street four young men filing out of an old car roared with laughter as they hurried into a tavern. The old house next door to the tavern was being torn down, and workmen were leaving for the day. When Dubuque had been a boy it had been a street of fine old mansions. Now these mansions had been turned into restaurants. Standing there he thought how fine it would be if someone who shared his appreciation of Ilona's quality could be at Muldoon's tonight: someone he could talk to later. There was only Gil. Smiling to himself, he thought about how she was a secret he shared with Gil, and he drove to Mr. Gilhooley's.

It was the beginning of the cocktail hour, and Gil was busy. Dubuque finally got him to come to the end of the bar, and in a low voice told him about his plan. "Not a word of it to anybody," he whispered. "I thought you yourself would want to drop in." Looking at him from a distance, Gil frowned, baffled, believing, yet wondering how it was that he believed that Dubuque knew he would some day tell Ilona's story.

"Thanks, Dubuque," he said finally. "Thanks. I won't breathe a word to anybody. Wait a minute. Judge Gibbons . . . No. Never mind about the Judge. I'll drop in."

Dubuque said, "What's this about the Judge?" But Gil moved away, and Dubuque, leaving, said, "What do I care about the Judge?"

Since he still regarded Ilona Tomory as one of his business enterprises, he said nothing to his wife about the evening ahead at Muldoon's. At dinner she asked if he had something on his mind. When he said no, nothing was worrying him, and laughed, she went on gossiping about the new neighbors, who amused her; they were university people who had installed "his" and "hers" sinks in their remodelled bathrooms. Then, for some reason that he could not understand, his club foot began to bother him; he wanted to get the heavy shoe off and have a nap. Sitting on the bed, he held the thick boot in his hands, wondering why it had felt so heavy. After a nap and a shower he put on his own three-piece dark suit. It was a quarter after nine, time to leave. Twenty-five minutes later he was in the car on Ilona's street. He stared for a long time at the little house, so similar on the outside to all the others in the row, before he got out.

She came to the door in a floor-length white gown with two thin shoulder straps, saying casually, "Hello, there." He had expected her to sound elated, or nervous, or excited. He was taken aback when she led him into the living room where she stood motionless off by herself in her white dress on the rich blue Chinese rug saying nothing. Indicating the chair he was to sit in, she sat down opposite him, remaining silent while he waited and wondered and wished he could see her whirl around in that long white dress on that blue rug. As she eyed him, her smile was faint and remote, as if he had broken some mood she was in.

"Well, are we ready, Ilona?" he asked. When she merely nodded without moving, he said sharply, "What's bothering you, Ilona? What's on your mind?"

"Oh, nothing, really," she said, shrugging. "While I was waiting I got to thinking, I suppose."

"Thinking what?"

"Did you read that piece in the papers about that great and famous old Paris dressmaker. What's her name?"

"I know who you mean."

"In her eighties."

"So?"

"A great life. This woman who had everything in the world of fame and fashion. Well, she was asked, if she had it to do over again, was there anything else she would rather have been, and, thinking it over, she said possibly, yes. She might have liked to have been a great courtesan. . . ."

"Well, well, well," Dubuque said with satisfaction as he stood up. "That's right, Ilona. Something unique, something famous, something like a dream." But her face changed. She was struggling against some new-found doubt about herself. "That's all right," she said. "But I never wanted to have a manager. A performer with a manager? Is that me? What am I? Do I want to be someone else?" But the look on Dubuque's face made her change again. Laughing, she said, "Oh, you should have come fifteen minutes earlier and not left me sitting here thinking," and she got up and did a whirl in her white dress on the blue rug.

"That's right," he said, holding her coat which had been on the chair. "Keep me guessing. Keep me guessing."

"No, here we go, Mr. Dubuque."

"Jay to you, I keep saying."

"You know what I've been calling you?"

"What?"

"Caliban."

"Which one?" he said, as if he knew.

"The one in the play."

"Oh, I thought you meant the one I know. The bookie," he said. "Well, I don't need to give you any instructions. I don't know how you cast your spell. Just feel like doing it, and you'll do it as soon as you stand up," and she said nothing, nothing at all, as they went out to the car.

"You're very good, Ilona," he went on. "But after all you're merely being introduced at Muldoon's. Nothing else to it," and though his eyes were on the road he knew she was looking at him with amusement.

"Just be myself," she said. "It's the easiest thing I do. Look, if this comes off tonight, I'll cook you a dinner. A real Hungarian dinner."

"You can cook?"

"I'm a great cook," she said. "I love cooking."

It was a dry, clear moonlit night, easy on her slippers and hair, and when he had parked the car and was crossing the street he became aware, for the first time, that she was at least an inch taller than he was, and he said, "Tall and regal, eh?" and she said, "It's the heels I'm wearing." At the entrance to Muldoon's he gave a kid who was juggling three balls, and dropping them, a dollar.

In the crowded lounge where many of the patrons

were still having dinner their reserved table was some thirty feet from the little stage where Jimmie Sykes fooled around with the keyboard as he always did in the hour following Chita's performance. It was a friendly lounge with an atmosphere of ease and a lot of well-off people who knew each other. Snatches of song came from some tables. The more the patrons drank, the more neighborly they became, as they would have done in a big private club.

"Not much like the Bradley lounge, eh?" Dubuque said.

"Oh, not so different," she said. "Here they have more money, that's all." But a little flush had come on her cheeks. She was getting keyed up. She hardly touched her drink, hardly heard him, didn't smile at his jokes, was actually tightening up. She worried him, and looking around he tried to spot Gil, hoping he could point him out to her.

"Maybe Gil couldn't get here," he said. "No. Maybe he's sitting out at the bar, waiting. I'm sure Gil's here. He must be."

And she, for her part, after looking all around, brightened, for there some five tables away was Judge Gibbons. He had had dinner here with a middle-aged lawyer, and now he stared at her intently and kept on till he caught her eye and held it for a long moment, held her eye till she smiled faintly. And then his own face lit up: just a meeting of the eyes, but a meeting of exhilarating serenity and warmth for him. Dubuque could not know what had happened, yet was aware that she had regained all her composure.

"See someone you know?" he asked.

"Judge Gibbons."

"Why, that's wonderful," he said thoughtfully. "Just the kind we're after."

"Ladies and gentlemen," Jimmie Sykes called, leaving the piano. "I'm told we have someone with us tonight you'd like to see . . . Ilona Tomory," and he started to clap his hands. "Please, Miss Tomory . . ."

Her coat draped on her shoulders, she stood up, all eyes turning to her. Jimmie Sykes kept clapping, then beckoning; and as people in crowds do, those at the tables, out of curiosity and led by Sykes, and liking what they saw of her, kept up the clapping. With a gracious little smile, so natural in its acceptance of their approval, she glided toward the little bandstand and the four steps. The faint smile accentuated her indulgent superiority. When Sykes whispered to her and she shook her head, preparing to leave, he touched her arm, coaxing her, and he sat down at the piano. Slipping off her coat near the piano, she did a thing then that made Dubuque grin with delight. A tall, cool princess now, in a white gown with two thin shoulder straps, she held the coat by the collar with her right hand, the long folds on the floor. Then she moved about eight feet, trailing the coat on the floor, creating an impression of superb untouchable elegance.

The spotlight that followed her to the stage had left the table in shadow, and Dubuque, moving quickly in the shadow, circled around the bandstand to get behind the curtain, knowing he only had two minutes before she would leave the stage. But if she faltered in that two minutes he would be there if he were needed. He got behind the curtain in time to hear her talk-sing, "Oh, the shark has . . . pearly teeth, dear . . ." And then, breaking off just as they had planned, she stood there, her eyes closed in a smiling dream, ready to bow, laugh, and go back to the table.

But then from a table to the left came a short, happy whoop. A half-drunken, thirty-five-year-old fair and handsome salesman, sitting with four men who had been drinking too much and finding each other very funny, dug his hand in his pocket, pulled out a handful of coins, and, laughing, tossed a quarter at Ilona's feet, then a penny, then another quarter. The coins rolled around her feet. There was utter silence. Abashed by the crowd's silence, the salesman shouted defensively, "It's a joke. She's from the Bradley lounge. A hooker from the Bradley lounge. The cream of the hooker crop. Aren't you, sweetie?"

As the coins rolled around her feet, there had been fury in Ilona's face, but at the words "Aren't you, sweetie?" her face changed. In the tilt of her head and her disdainful stillness, there was a dignity that abashed the whole lounge. Even the bouncer, who now had his hand on the heckler's shoulder, stared at her, making no move, held for the moment by her silent dignity.

Then Dubuque, coming from behind the curtain, and crossing the little platform in front of her, took the four steps down to the floor, and, moving deliberately, his step even, his heavy shoulders hunched up a little, his chin tucked in, he limped by all the front tables to the fair handsome salesman's table and without a word smacked him hard on the face.

The startled bouncer didn't move. No one in the room said a word. No one moved as the salesman stood up, tall and willowy and four inches taller than Dubuque. As he stepped out from the table he put his hands up, his left out correctly, his right against his face, looking like a picture from a boy's book on the noble art of self-defence. He feinted at Dubuque with his left. Weaving a little, Dubuque threw two hooks, a left and a right, hooking like a pro. When the tall young man went down, rolling over on his back, Dubuque turned without a word and made his way toward Ilona, who had been standing near the piano, motionless, watching. Every-body in the room was standing. No one, not even his half-drunk friends, offered the salesman any sympathy. The bouncer tried to drag him to his feet. Muldoon, who had been called from his office, a cheated man, red-faced and angry, tried to get to Dubuque. Men at the tables who knew Muldoon grabbed at his arm, question-ing him.

Ilona hadn't moved till the salesman put up his hands and got decked by Dubuque. Frightened now, she left the little platform and, with people staring at her, blocking the way, she tried to get out of the room, till Dubuque got her by the arm. "It's all right," he said grimly. "It's all right. You're not running out, you hear? Nobody wants you to run out. It'll be all right. Sit down at your table. Come on, sit down."

"You bungler," she said fiercely. "You stupid bungler. I knew I shouldn't come here. You got me into this." Jerking her arm loose, she got two paces away, but then grabbing at her he got her by the shoulder.

"Ilona," he said savagely, "you're not running out of here like this."

As she tried to knock his hand off her shoulder, he hung on. His fingers were on the shoulder strap of the dress, and when she kept jerking her arm away, the dress tore. He had only a big strip from the white dress in his hand as she got away.

She rushed by the bar stool where Johnny Sills had been sitting in his camel's-hair overcoat. He jumped up, slipping off the coat. He called, "Lady, lady. Wait," and hurried after her. Her own mink coat lay on the stage floor.

Hearing nothing, seeing nothing, Dubuque got her coat from the stage and rushed after her. When he was getting his own coat at the checkroom, Gil, who had been standing near the bar, called angrily, "Dubuque, for Christ's sake . . ." But Dubuque couldn't bear to recognize him. He kept on going.

Gil called out again, standing in the doorway, blocking the patrons who were leaving. "Gil," Judge Gibbons said, taking his arm. The middle-aged colleague of the Judge was getting the coats. Pale and hard-eyed now, the Judge was unduly outraged, unduly shaken, unduly hurt. "Gil," he whispered, looking around. "Why was she here with that notorious thug?"

"Well, he can arrange these things," Gil said.

"It was an assault on her, a violent assault. I saw him."

"Sure it was."

"Where's Muldoon? He should lay a charge. I'll tell him so."

"Don't. Muldoon won't press the charge."

"It's a citizen's obligation. He'll have to."

"Judge . . . keep out of it, okay?"

"But that thug . . ."

"I don't know, Judge," Gil said awkwardly. "Maybe Dubuque just can't help being Dubuque. Still . . . I don't know. Dubuque never loses his head. He can't afford to. . . . Well, there's your friend with your coat," and he added in a whisper, "Keep out of it, okay?"

"Yes, I must not be a fool," the Judge muttered, turning away to let his friend help him with his coat.

Out on the street in bright winter moonlight, Dubuque, now some thirty feet from the entrance, looked so wild he alarmed three passing girls who were laughing and trying to sing in harmony. When these girls were out of the way, Dubuque could see Ilona and Johnny Sills twenty paces ahead, Ilona in his coat, the big loose coat almost touching the sidewalk. Sills turned, taking her arm, coming back a few steps toward the hotel, as if they had thoughts of returning and getting her coat. When they saw Dubuque, Sills came striding toward him. "All right, fellow," he said. "She wants her coat."

"I'll give her her coat. Out of my way."

"She told me to get her coat."

"Let her tell me."

"Keep away from her, you clown."

"I warn you, keep your nose out of this, buster."

"You belong in burlesque, you clown. She wants her coat."

"I'm giving it to her," and as Dubuque called "Ilona", trying to brush by, Sills shouted, "She said keep away," and grabbed at the coat and hung on. They both tugged. Dubuque heard the skins tear. "You bastard," he said viciously. Shooting out his arm, Sills caught Dubuque with the heel of his hand, caught him on the side of the head, spinning him around, but as Dubuque lurched, spinning, he swung his good heavy, deadly boot at Sills's leg, catching him just below the knee. Sills went down, but in falling he wrapped his big arm around Dubuque's left leg, trying to drag him down, too. Then Dubuque kicked him in the head. Sills lay very still.

"No! No!" cried Ilona, running toward them, and as Sills's arm came up, his hand reaching for her, Dubuque could think only of a police car, and of the police finding him, Jay Dubuque, bending over Sills. So he backed away, back toward the hotel, telling himself that Ilona, seeing Sills rolling on his knees, trying to get up, would believe he was all right and would come after him, for as Dubuque hurried away he couldn't imagine her going anywhere without the coat. But when he looked back, she was still on her knees beside Sills, trying to help him sit on the curb. Seeing a taxi approaching, she stepped out to the road, waving both arms. In Sills's big camel's-hair coat she looked ridiculous. The taxi stopped. She helped Sills to his feet, but he was leaning on her so heavily she staggered. The taxi driver got out and helped her guide Sills into the taxi. After making a U-turn, the taxi headed down the street.

Gripping the coat tightly, Dubuque, out on the road, followed the taxi's red tail-light with his eyes, followed it across an intersection and past the gas station till the cab turned and came to a stop in front of an apartment house near a hotel.

Dubuque's heart was pounding so heavily he couldn't think clearly; he couldn't feel like himself, he couldn't feel he had any authority over anything. It was necessary to get back his authority. The first thing to do was to relax his grip on the coat and let it fall loosely over his arm. He did this. Then crossing the road he got into his car, drove the short distance down the street, and with the coat on his arm entered the apartment house. Sills's name was on a mailbox: Sills, on the third floor. But as he was about to press the button, he grew thoughtful and drew on his wisdom. If he rang, a voice, Sills's or hers, would say in the tube, "Who is it?" Why should they open the door? They might even call the police. So he returned to the car, where he tried to relax, his eyes on the apartment entrance.

But while he watched he began to suffer a strange remorse. He couldn't cope with this remorse. "So I'm sorry. So I'll tell her I'm sorry," he said aloud, but he couldn't understand his growing pain. Fleeing from the remorse, he turned angrily on her for remaining in the apartment with Sills, the anger fed by an awareness that Sills possessed resources he didn't have himself. Not only did Sills have money, or a proximity to money, he had a fine education; he had travelled; he had imagination, too, and as he had shown in that conversation at the bar, he had his own world of wonders just as good as those Hungarian wonders Ilona shared at home with her father and mother. And Sills was big and strong, and he didn't have a club foot. Having her in his thoughts, seeing her there beside him, Dubuque said, "I know what you're doing right now. Nursing him. Bandaging his goddamned head. Down beside him soothing him. Comforting him. That look on your face, and he eats it up, and he sits up, and then off come your clothes. You know how to take him and heal him. That's you. Not a hooker. A healer! Right? Right. The hooker healer. Come, come, come on to me. Why, you're as crazy as your father and mother."

With the car engine turned off, the heat had gone and it was getting cold. Shivering, he became more like himself. The fact was, he told himself, he had her coat, and he was sure she couldn't see herself in the winter snow without that coat. Relaxing, he drove home.

15

WHEN HE WAS IN HIS OFFICE THE NEXT AFTERNOON making some phone calls, and the door opened and Sills walked in, he knew how right he had been about the coat. But he was surprised that Sills, approaching him so calmly, looked so much bigger. He had on a loose expensive black coat. Under the tweed hat, and well back of the right ear, was a bandage over the black hair. Sills had the air of a polite casual visitor about to deal with a stranger. Since he had just removed his heavy boot, Dubuque couldn't bring himself to stand up. All morning he had been walking up and down in a hotel room dealing with twelve bookies who were contributing to the slush fund that would guarantee warnings of police raids on their establishments. There had also been arguments about how to eliminate three bookies who wouldn't come into the organization. His foot had been aching from all the pacing and the standing. If he had stood up now, looking so lopsided, only one shoe on, he would have felt he had no authority.

"Miss Tomory asked me to see you about her coat and pick it up," Sills said quietly. Then, seeing the coat which Dubuque had brought to the office lying on the red leather chair in the corner, he said, "Ah, I see you have it here."

"Yeah, I have it there," Dubuque said, hobbling quickly over to the coat. Startled by the stockinged foot and the lopsided gait, Sills drew back, watching, while Dubuque, the coat on his arm, hobbled over to the door. Opening it, he pointed to the hall. "I've heard nothing from Miss Tomory about giving you the coat. I'm busy. There's the door. Now beat it."

"I'm here for Miss Tomory. I'm here."

"So you say."

"I've just left Miss Tomory."

"So you say. I've no instructions from her," Dubuque said, and, draping the coat on the back of his own desk chair, he sat down.

"What do I have to do?" Sills asked. "Get a cop?"

"Sure. Get a cop. Get a fire truck. Get yourself an ambulance."

"I see," Sills said, his face flushing. "The Man, eh? You're The Man. Don't fool with The Man. I'll get my leg broken or my head smashed in."

"People say the craziest things, don't they, buster?"

"Look, Mr. Man, from now on you're to keep away from Ilona."

"Who says so?"

"If you don't I'll come after you. Yeah," Sills said quietly as he approached the desk. "You know, I could pick you up and throw you out that window." Though

Dubuque grinned, he felt suddenly wary, but not out of physical fear. It was just that he had suddenly felt a power in Sills that had nothing to do with the family money, or the education, or the faraway places and the dreamy talk: no, the fear came from a recognition of some mysterious hard core in Sills, something in him that could hold Ilona, something Sills himself would have words for.

Unable to understand his fear, Dubuque lashed out viciously. "You're a meddler. Nothing to do but meddle. What are you doing putting your snotty nose in my business? What do you know about me or Ilona? You're just a nuisance, just a fucking nuisance. Now beat it. I'm busy!"

"The coat. Do you mind?"

"Yeah, I mind," Dubuque said, leaning forward, the palms of both hands planted magisterially on the desk. As they eyed each other steadily, Sills's face became cruel and hard. "Yeah. I owe you one, don't I?" he said softly. Picking up the heavy metal ash tray there on the desk, he swung it, and when Dubuque, startled, ducked, Sills pounded the tray down on the back of Dubuque's hand lying flat on the desk.

"Oh, Christ," Dubuque yelled, doubling up. In his pain he could hardly see, but he was aware of Sills coming around the desk to get the coat. Right under his eye on the floor was the heavy surgical boot. Grabbing it, he flung it with all his strength, hitting Sills on the back of the neck. Big and all as Sills was, he staggered, thrown off balance. Jumping up, and using his shoulder and barrel chest to catch him off balance, Dubuque butted him toward the door, and before Sills could recover his balance he gave him a violent shove out to the hall, then locked the door. Leaning against the door, his eyes closed, he felt the numbness in his hand being replaced by an excruciating pain, the pain growing as Sills rattled the doorknob and pounded at the glass. Then there was the sound of voices in the hall. One of the next-door lawyers had come out of his office and was talking to Sills. The voices moved away. In a few minutes came a polite knock on the door. "Mr. Dubuque—are you all right, Mr. Dubuque?"

Keeping the injured hand behind his back, Dubuque opened the door. "It's all right," he said to the concerned lawyer, a sandy-haired middle-aged man with freckles. "Just a big drunk, wanting money. I had to throw him out."

"Good God, I thought he was getting ready to tear down the door."

"It's all right."

"Some years ago I had to throw a drunk out of my office. Got him out all right, then found I had dislocated my shoulder. Very painful."

"Yeah, they can do a lot of damage," Dubuque said, still hiding his hand. "A panhandler."

"Panhandling?"

"Just panhandling."

"The gall of the man. A well-dressed panhandler. Well, it's a serious matter when we're not safe in our own offices. The street is one thing. The other day, out there by the liquor store, when I was going in I gave a panhandler a quarter. When I came out he was right back at me, scowling and wanting another quarter."

"That's right. Everybody wants a handout these days."

"The other day a man came into my office. Well-dressed—like your man. I gave him a dollar and, do you know, he cursed me. Literally cursed me—said I could afford a lot more than a dollar. Well, I admire you for being able to throw your man out. I really do. You're sure you're all right?"

"I'm all right," Dubuque said. "Thanks. Thanks very much." Closing the door, he limped back to the desk, picking up his boot on the way. Rocking back and forth in his swivel chair, his eyes closed, he nursed the pain in his hand, telling himself a bone couldn't be broken, because he could move the fingers a little. The pain sharpened his perceptions, and it became plain that Sills, the son of a bitch, really had hold of Ilona. How had Sills, unlike all the others, got to her? That was the question. "Oh, Jesus," he muttered, closing his hand slowly and trembling with rage. "We'll see, we'll see," he kept repeating. Yet nothing could be done—unless he understood the nature of Sills's hold on her. I'm a fool. What is she in it for, he thought. What are they all in it for? The money. Where does any woman go? Where the money is.

Looking again at his hand, he got up and headed for the washroom, hoping that on the way he would have one of his profound hunches. After bathing his hand and having no hunch about anything, he went down to the drugstore and got some surgical tape. He remembered he had some appointments. He had to see his tax consultant, then get back to the office by five o'clock to call a client, Mr. Eisendrath, in Detroit.

All the street lights were on by the time he got back to his office and put in his Detroit call. "Dubuque is the name," he said to the receptionist. "Tell him to call Dubuque. No, I'm not calling from Dubuque. No, this *is* Dubuque. I'm Dubuque. Not in Dubuque. Edmund J. Dubuque. God damn you, you silly woman!" he yelled. "Just take this number and call me." A little later when the telephone rang he grabbed it. "Dubuque here."

"Mr. Dubuque . . ."

"Yeah. Oh, Ilona."

"You said it was necessary I call you," she began curtly. "I understand you wanted word from me if you were to give Mr. Sills my coat."

"Was that such a foolish thing?" he asked mildly. "Who is this man? Just a man from last night, a man off the streets."

"I asked him to get the coat. He was there for me."

"How did I know? If you had called me, if you had said, there's a man coming around to get my coat. . . . Why didn't you call?"

"I'm calling now. You need some authority, you said. All right, you have my authority. Understand: give my coat to Mr. Sills."

"I can't," he lied.

"What do you mean, you can't?"

"The lining is torn, Ilona. I took it to a furrier," he lied.

"You took it to a furrier. For God's sake, why can't you mind your own business?" she said angrily. But then, after a long hesitation, "Just the lining?"

"Just the lining," he said. "And listen, Ilona. I want to apologize. For what I did at Muldoon's I want to apologize. Look . . ." then he stammered, fumbling words, trying hard to find the right words, hardly understanding what he wanted to say and actually was saying. "That crowd, see? Are you there, Ilona. I was hurting. I couldn't stand the hurt. I mean the hurt was coming from you—all from you. I had to end the hurt." He waited, but she said nothing. "All right. Never mind, I'll get the coat to you," he said.

"When?" she asked.

"As soon as possible. Maybe tomorrow. How about tomorrow?"

"Can it be called for?"

"How can I say when?"

"Look," she began, her voice sounding younger. "As you know, that's really my mother's coat, and she doesn't know it's not in the house. She talks about going to the doctor's tomorrow, or the next day."

"Don't worry. You'll get the coat, Ilona," and he grabbed the coat and hurried out.

16

IN THE EARLY DARK ON COLLEGE STREET, DUBUQUE came across the road, the coat on his arm, on his way to Freeman, the furrier. He liked passing the Italian shoe shops, the bright Italian food stores and fruit markets, and he liked the way the Italian boys congregated on the sidewalk, even with the weather getting colder. And he had always liked going in to see Freeman, who had known him since the old days and had great respect for his success.

The store was a disreputable-looking place, but Albert Freeman, who had a great reputation in the business, was now a well-off man. To the left of the entrance was a long rack of choice second-hand coats. Freeman, who had an arrangement with Levine Furs, got these coats and worked on them himself. Untidy though his shop was, customers came from all over town, and no woman, no matter how rich, impressed him. He knew how good he was.

He was ready to close the shop for the day. At the sound of the opening door his Great Dane came through the curtain that screened the workroom from the store. Wagging his tail in recognition, the big dog kept barking happily till Freeman appeared.

A grey-bearded man of sixty, he squinted hard through thick glasses. When he had been a boy working long hours to support his mother, he had ruined his eyes reading in bed by flashlight when he was supposed to be sleeping. "Jay, my boy, Jay," he cried, beaming. They embraced. They laughed. They were old friends. Freeman had a lovely deep, warm laugh. Once a month Jay came for dinner with Freeman and his daughter, Paula. Paula was pretty, and wanted to design clothes, so as often as possible Jay introduced her to men in the fashion business who came to the hotels. He owed it to Albert Freeman.

In his whole life, Jay had had only two real teachers: the Cookie Lady, and this man, Freeman, who seemed to have under analysis everything going on in every country in the world. He would explain national figures in his warm low voice over many cups of coffee. Once, trying to talk to Dubuque about Russian literature, he cried, "What's the matter with you, Jay? You have natural insights. Get beyond your own nose. But maybe you'll never understand these men, and never understand your own life till you've rolled in the gutter yourself. Nobody does. I've been in the gutter, Jay. Have you?"

"Me? The gutter? What the hell, I don't know," Jay said, and, laughing, changed the subject.

Now he clapped his old friend on the shoulder. "How's Paula?" he asked.

"Paula's a problem now. A pretty unmarried girl is always a problem. I want her to go to school."

"Let her go to school."

"She wants money. A girl at school should not have too much money, I say. Well, what have you got for me?" and he reached for the coat, moving into the back of the store to his workbench.

"A skin got torn, Albert," Jay said. "More than one tear, as you can see. The lining's torn, too. Don't ask me how it happened. I was to blame," he said, stroking the head of the big dog that leaned against his leg, listening attentively. This dog, Freeman had declared, was a better burglar alarm than anything on the market.

"Once upon a time this was a real coat," Freeman said. But as he held the fur up, scrutinizing the skins, his voice changed. "Jay," he said in an outraged tone, "this fur is so dry! The skins are so dry! What do you expect me to do?"

"Just sew up the tears. And the lining," Jay said. "Put a new lining in—something in that nice rich brown color. What's the matter?" he asked, because Freeman had stepped back, aghast.

"Jay," Freeman said, turning in exasperation from the bench. "What is this, Jay? Is it right you should come to me? What am I?" He was growing outraged. "You bring this coat to me. Nobody could sew those skins. They are so old, so brittle, so dry they couldn't take a stitch. Those skins. They're taped. See! Under the lining it's all tape. For God's sake, have a look, man." He had opened up the lining a little. Now he opened more and more, finally pulling all the fur clean off the lining. Long lines of tape supported all the seams. Some of the tapes looked very old, and by this time were so tightly stuck to the skins they could never be removed. Other more recent strips of tape were not holding as well.

"Well?" Freeman demanded, waiting. Suddenly he

laughed. It was his good, warm, earth-loving laugh, yet the warmth of this laugh, the down-to-earth sensible richness of the laugh, hurt Dubuque painfully. Staring blankly at the spread-out taped-up skins he thought of Ilona and her mother and father. The Tomorys. They all knew the coat was like this. They knew all about each other. While Freeman, growing impatient for an answer, shrugged, waving his hands, Dubuque felt he was hearing a story that could only have a bad ending.

Finally he got out his cigar case, and, taking out two fine Cuban cigars, offered one to Albert. He lit Albert's cigar, then his own. "Tape up the coat, Albert," he said quietly.

"Jay. What am I? You insult me."

"Can't you tape it, Albert?"

"I'm a furrier. I'm a first-class furrier, Jay. You have always respected my work. I don't do such things."

"I'm in a mess, Albert," he said. "A real mess." He was bewildered by the strength of Albert's professional pride. But he thought he could con Albert. He knew phrases that always had magic for Albert, his teacher, his philosophical friend. "Albert," he said carefully. "You're a human being, and I'm a human being. You used to say to me, making exciting talk about what was going on, 'A human being, Jay. Do you know what that means? Does anybody stop today to wonder what that means?' Well, this girl who owns this coat has an importance for me. It can turn out to be a big importance. But look, old friend, it's really her mother's coat. You see, Albert, I think it's a kind of family coat. I think the goddamned thing has to be there in the house for them, looking right. The girl wears it at night. I don't know what the hell is bigger for them than the look of the thing. God damn it, that girl is expecting me to bring that coat to her looking good, and I suppose some sleight of hand, and not a furrier, can bring that off now. But, if you want to do it, you can do it, Albert. I don't care what it costs. Put someone on it tonight. Overtime. Time and a half for overtime."

"My poor man," Albert said. "What's got into you? Look—buy a coat. Come back tomorrow and I'll show you something that's a steal. Let us not insult ourselves." Half angry, he was walking Jay to the door. It was closing time.

While talking, Albert had opened the door, and so the Great Dane walked out. "Thor," Albert called angrily. The dog, who was never free of the leash on the street, turned, looked at Albert solemnly, then hurried off along the street. "Oh, my God," Albert said, "I'm in trouble," and went to dash out in his vest and rolled-up sleeves.

"I'll get him. Stay here. It's my fault," Dubuque said. "No trouble."

The big dog, twenty yards ahead, sniffed at a post, lifted his leg, then trotted along. "Thor," Dubuque called commandingly. "Thor." The dog did turn, waiting till Jay had limped to only ten feet behind, then trotting on ahead. "Thor, Thor, you bastard," Dubuque shouted. Again the dog turned, let him catch up, and again trotted on, this time toward three women coming along the street who stopped, stiffening in fright. A trusting little boy came up to the dog, his hand out. Scared, Dubuque shouted, "Keep away, son." The dog moved away, just leading Dubuque on, knowing exactly where he was.

Realizing this could go on for miles, Dubuque tried whistling, he tried a wheedling tone, but he couldn't get within reach of the dog till they came to a fruit store where a young man, who was carrying a giant toy teddy bear, stood looking at fruit in the window. The big dog, stopping at the teddy bear, raised his leg. The young man jerked the teddy bear away. The dog barked, waited, and growled. Dropping the teddy bear, the young man ran into the store. By this time, Dubuque, catching up, was able to grab the dog's choke-chain. The dog looked at him agreeably with his soft brown eyes. "You big frightening son of a bitch," Dubuque scolded him, and kept on scolding while the dog trotted along willingly back to the store.

"Thank you, Jay. Thank you," Albert said. "You see, the cops have told me not to let him out on the street without a leash." Dubuque said nothing. Taking the choke-chain himself, Albert grew embarrassed. They were two old friends, silent at a door that was about to be closed. "I was watching you go along the street," Albert said. "Limping and hurrying and pleading, you were. A nice thing for me to see, Jay," he went on awkwardly. "As you say, before we're anything else, we're human beings. Before I am a furrier, what am I? A human being. Yes, I said to myself, watching you, 'Jay's got money. It's not money here. It's something else. Must be some little human thing about that coat which makes it important to him.' So what the hell, Jay. I'll stick it all together for you. Not as a furrier. As an artist. I'll make it look good with a new lining."

"Thanks, Albert," Dubuque said.

"Good night, Jay."

"Albert, I owe you one," Jay said. "Good night."

His relief, buoying him up, lasted through the evening, which was a busy one. He had promised his wife that he would do some shopping. The big stores were open at night. After his shopping, he had an appointment in his office with a Mrs. Weldon, a plump, pretty woman whose husband had lost his executive job. He had a drink with Mrs. Weldon. She was touched by the respect he offered her. After dealing with her, he had a few phone calls to make, some notes to write, and it was eleven o'clock before he was in his car on the way home.

His street was in very bright moonlight and when he turned his car into the lane thirty yards away from his house, it was as bright as day. He got out of his car to open the garage doors; then, walking back to the car he thought he heard a sound. It was nothing. A tomcat wailed, then came the screeching of two cats, and one cat, leaping down from the garage roof, ran down the lane. After he had put his car in the garage and was closing the doors, he got a blow on the back of his head, the strangest feeling he had ever had. The black sky came pressing down on his mind, the blackness coming lower and lower, then lifting a little just before wiping him out. He thought he might be having a stroke.

Then the heavy blackness began to lift a little more, and he could see two men coming at him. They pinned him against the garage door. He tried feebly to kick out with his deadly boot. "Son of a bitch," one of them said and hit him on the jaw. The other one held him as he turned his face away to press it against the cold door. They hit him in the belly. Again and again he was hit in the belly, and each time he moaned he was hit again. "Okay," the voice said. The sound of running feet was in his ears as he slid to the ground.

Gagging, he vomited, then tried to sit up. Finally, when he felt the coldness in the ground through his pants, he tried to get up, and kept trying till he made it. Taking one deep breath, then another, and then giving a terrible sigh, he looked up at the sky and the bright moon. "This, this," he protested to the moon. "What did I do? All I wanted was to give a girl a far better life than she had, where she could go on doing what she wants to do, but with comfort and style and money and admiration and respect. And I get this."

Struggling to his feet he asked himself who paid those guys. Spagnola? Ah, no. Frankie could pay a couple of hundred dollars for the job but he would be too scared. Those Montreal guys? But he didn't want it to be them. It had to be young Sills, who could easily get hold of the money for the job. It had to be Sills. His whole body came alive with the satisfaction he got out of blaming Sills. Cursing, he began to dust off his coat. The main thing was that his wife should not see him in a condition that would tell her he had been beaten up. She couldn't imagine anyone being able to beat him up.

17

WHEN WORD OF DUBUQUE'S REMARKABLE PERFOR-
mance at The Muldoon got around the Bradley lounge,
no one dared mention it to him. Three nights in a row he
had come into the lounge, nights when he waited to hear
from Albert that the coat had been repaired, although
Albert had told him it would take at least four days to
get the skins held together properly. Whenever Dubuque
came into the lounge, he had one of his henchmen go to
"the block" and ask if any one of the girls had seen
Ilona. None had seen her.

Since his hand still hurt him, he kept it hidden. No
one asked him how he had got the welt on his jaw, and it
was as if they were all trained never to ask about his
marks of violence. People had built up the Muldoon
story, making Dubuque out to have been more violent
and more contemptuous of the Muldoon patrons than he
had been, and in doing so had built up their own awe of
him. He didn't care what they thought; he was sure of
his following. They were his own people.

The only one at the Bradley who wanted to question him was Gil, who sometimes caught a glimpse of him through the lattice grill. Gil wanted Dubuque to come into the bar so he could talk to him about Ilona. Each night before Gil fell asleep she kept coming into his thoughts, stirring his imagination, and he knew now that no matter what he thought of Dubuque and his criminal life, Dubuque had become part of Ilona's story as he would tell it. His intuition told him, too, that even though Dubuque's interest in her seemed to be ruthlessly commercial, she must have some other powerful hold on him.

Early on the fourth night Dubuque drove to Ilona's house with the repaired coat in a handsome purple box. It was snowing, but softly, peacefully, the way it should be snowing at this time of year. Her house was the only house on the street with the snow already shovelled, and she herself came to the door.

"Come in," she said quietly, and under that globe of golden light on the ceiling, she made him feel so much like an utter stranger that he was surprised that she had let him in.

"It's very good of you," she said, taking the box. "But you didn't need to bring it yourself."

"Like I told you," he said, wary of her, "they don't deliver at night and I knew you wanted it. How is your mother?"

"I don't know. Not well at all. Thanks for sending her the roses." She indicated the roses in the antique vase.

"I heard she wasn't well and I knew she would like roses."

"Yes. Always roses," she said, and then, troubled, she went on, "These setbacks are so hard on her. Thank heavens the doctor is worried too, now. He's had us filling her with iron pills for her blood, but he's sure she'll have to go to the hospital for some real blood tests. I hope he gets in tonight. Well. . . ." She sighed. She did not ask him to take off his coat and have a glass of wine and a biscuit as he had imagined she might, but when she walked into the living room with the box, he followed, watching her take the coat out and hold it at arm's length, looking at the new lining. "A beautiful new lining—why, that's lovely," she said. "You didn't need to have that done." As she folded the coat he saw her glance quickly at the skins.

"You've paid for this, Jay. Just tell me what it cost."

"Not much," he said. "You don't owe me, Ilona. I owe you."

"I'd like to pay you. Really I would."

"And how would I feel? Come on. Give me a break."

"Well, if it helps you to feel easier about things."

"Just a little thing, but it helps."

"I see," she said, and when she sat down with the coat on her lap, indicating that she expected him to sit down, too, he felt there was some judgment of him forming in her eyes, and he hoped she remembered his fumbling, painful, mixed-up apology.

"You're okay, Jay," she said, but as her eyes held his, he grew upset. In her eyes was a caressing sympathy for him just as he was, a kind of solace so strange to his nature it hurt. He shifted his eyes away, concentrating on a thick red lighted candle in a tall wrought-iron holder in the corner of the lovely room.

"Well, who shovelled the snow?" he asked.

"I did."

"You did?"

"Sure I did."

"I bet you made it look good doing it."

"Well, there's one thing I'll say for you."

"What's that?"

"You know how to make a woman feel like a woman."

"Hey—I really respect women."

"In your crazy way, yes, I think you do," she said, frowning. "I think you really put a high price on them." Liking this, he began to relax and take his time.

"How's your hand?" she asked suddenly.

"My hand?" Startled, he looked at his hand, knowing she must be aware of what had happened. "Look," he began awkwardly, "I couldn't let a guy I didn't know have your coat. These scholars. They go berserk, you know. . . ."

"Keep your voice down, please," she said glancing at the stairs.

"I'm sorry," he said.

"I mean, we're hoping Mother will fall asleep. My father's trying to lull her asleep."

"I'm sorry," he said. "Well, look, Ilona," he began, believing he now knew how to handle her. "It may turn out that young Sills is a good one for you to know," and he leaned a little closer so she could hear every word. "That crazy business the other night . . . when I hit that guy . . . it takes a couple of days to come down to earth. But look, Johnny Sills may not be able to forget you. That's good, eh?"

"Is it so hard to believe?" she asked, smiling faintly.

"No, I'm sure of it."

"Yes, I think you are."

"Now, here's the thing, Ilona. The Sillses have a lot

of money, okay. Young Sills, of course, hasn't got any. That's okay. All he has to do is kiss his old man's ass and he's back in business again, chasing those temples and angels and the books, all the stuff he can only chase now at Muldoon's. Soon he'll have the money to pay for these tickets to nowhere. Handle him right, Ilona. It's what we want. Right? And he'll be a very good client. Right? Just the kind of client we're after."

"Are you sure of this, too?" she asked, and her smile troubled him.

"He really likes you, doesn't he?"

"I think so."

"A friend. A good, rich, generous friend. I know you can never be too sure of such friends," he went on, leaning back, half closing his eyes as if offering a purely objective judgment out of the wisdom of his whole life. "For what it's worth, Ilona, I'd say Johnny Sills is one of those half-wild, selfish guys—those maniacs—who are half-tame pussycats too, always wanting to be cuddled in someone's lap. At the heart of the guy there'll be something soft we can count on."

"Soft?" she asked quietly. "A scholar . . . who has the guts to blow up his whole world—as he did—and walk out?"

"Walk out where? To what? To Muldoon's bar. Sure, a likeable, mixed-up boy. But we have to play him right." But he saw that instead of bringing her down to earth, he had only made her dreamily reflective, with her downward glance fixed on the shimmering blue Chinese rug. Then, as she made a little pattern with the toe of her elegant shoe on the rug, her face changed, and in it now was a new serenity, and she could have forgotten that he was there. Clearing his throat gruffly, coughing ostentatiously, he glanced at the stairs. "Come off it, Ilona," he said roughly. "What was so different about it the other night?"

"Different? Different from what?"

"All the others?" and he tried a grin. "Look, come off it, I know the way it went. In that goddamned apartment, with Sills banged up like he was, it was only natural you'd be sympathetic and want to show the guy he'd never hit anything as real as you. Don't tell me you didn't get into bed with him."

"I got into bed with him. Of course."

"All sympathy and compassion. Yeah, that's you, Ilona. This rare intimacy."

"You know what he said?" she asked dreamily.

"What?"

"It was sacramental."

"Sacramental? What's that? A religious thing."

"Yes. A religious thing."

Perplexed, he waited a moment. "Fucking is fucking, Ilona," he said profoundly. "How can it be a religious thing?"

"If fucking can't be a religious thing," she asked softly, "what can be religious?"

Taken aback, he pondered, hoping to say something bright and amusing. "You've got me," he said finally.

But she stood up, alert, listening, tense. "What was that?"

18

SOMEONE WAS STUMBLING AROUND IN THE UPSTAIRS hall, then they heard a thump, the sound of someone falling, the murmur of voices so low they couldn't be heard, and then Mr. Tomory cried out, "Ilona!" Tossing the coat at a chair, she ran to the stairs. "I'll leave," Dubuque called, but when she merely waved, a downward motion of her hand, he wasn't sure whether she wanted him to go or stay and help her. Remaining in the hall, he listened, waiting, judging that Mrs. Tomory must have fallen in the hall, and that Ilona and her father were now helping her into the bedroom. For nearly ten minutes there was only the murmur of the two voices, Ilona's and her father's. Finally, Ilona, pale and distraught, came rushing down the stairs. "Can I help in any way?" he asked.

As she hurried along the narrow hall to the kitchen, she called over her shoulder, "He was helping her to the bathroom, and then she vomited. I'm sure it's blood.

Blood. Dark-brown stuff. All over the bathroom floor." Coming back from the kitchen with a pail and a mop she hurried up the stairs, and as her legs vanished he called, "Is that doctor coming?" He felt like a brash intruder. Taking a few steps up the stairs, each step giving him more confidence, he couldn't forget that this isolated family guarded their private matters as carefully as they did the hidden wonders of their home.

From where he stood at the top of the stairs in the richly carpeted narrow hall, he could see Ilona in the bathroom mopping the floor. By the door was the pail, now half full of water mixed with brownish ropy stuff. In the bathroom the brownish stains on the floor tiles were vanishing under Ilona's mop. "I've seen lots of people vomit," he said, "and that doesn't look like vomit. Ilona, look, my car is outside. If she can walk—if she did walk from here to the bedroom—maybe your father and I could get her downstairs and into the car. I can get to a hospital emergency in ten minutes."

Stiff and still, holding the mop handle in both hands, her head back as always, she said, "I knew you'd help if you could." But her hands had begun to shake. Swallowing hard, still trying to look like a fine lady, she said, "Come on," and led him into the small bedroom. It had a grand antique bed, and a floor covered wall-to-wall with one pale-blue and white rug, and there were two pale-blue bedroom chairs. "Dad," she said. "Mr. Dubuque is here. He can help maybe."

"Good evening, Mr. Dubuque. Yes, I knew you were here." Though his grey hair was badly mussed and his shirt sleeves were rolled up, he made a courtly bow that seemed to help him in his distress. It helped him to believe that while he could make this bow everything was going to be all right, and he turned to his wife, hidden under the bed covers except for her forehead and some wild strands of grey hair, as if he hoped she might sit up and smile now a visitor was in the house.

"Dad, listen," Ilona said. "If Mother has the strength to stand up—she has, hasn't she?—we could get right down to the emergency in Mr. Dubuque's car."

"I don't know," her father said helplessly. "I don't know." Bending over the bed, Ilona said, "Mother, could you move, do you think you could move?"

"Ilona," her mother whispered.

"Mother—Mother," Ilona pleaded.

Finally her mother whispered, "I'm so cold, oh, so cold," and then they saw how she still shivered under the blankets.

"She should be in a hospital, Mr. Tomory," Dubuque said.

"Surely we can warm her," Mr. Tomory said, as if he couldn't bear to think of the hospital. Then Ilona, who had run to her own bedroom, returned, her arms filled with blankets which she spread on the bed. "Now she'll be all right," Mr. Tomory said confidently. Yet as he stood in silence at the foot of the bed, he suddenly looked very much alone, and Dubuque again felt like a stranger.

Mrs. Tomory tried to speak to Ilona, who was stroking her head. She couldn't speak. Her teeth chattering, she tried to clench her jaw. "I'm calling an ambulance," Dubuque said, and he hurried downstairs to the telephone he had seen in the corner by the stairs. While he was dialling, Mr. Tomory came running downstairs to the hall cupboard, from which he gathered his own winter overcoat and two other coats and hurried back upstairs. "In twenty minutes. It'll be here in twenty minutes," Dubuque called, following Mr. Tomory.

Ilona and Mr. Tomory had spread the overcoats over the bed, and now Mr. Tomory, looking decisive and competent, said, "Everything will be all right now, Ilona. I don't know what this is. But the thing was to get her warm, and we're getting her warm." Yet her teeth still chattered. "It'll be all right now, Terezia. It'll be all right now," he said, and he actually smiled, reassuring himself, but further distressing Ilona.

Clearing his throat importantly, Dubuque said, "She must have lost a lot of blood. Too much blood," and then, waving his hands, "Why have I still got my own coat on?" and he began to take it off. But Ilona, who had been staring intently at her mother, cried, "I'll warm her," and ran downstairs. While she was gone, Mr. Tomory, his hand under the blankets on his wife's ankle, said, "Ah, there, I'm sure she's getting warmer. Yes, sir, yes, sir. The circulation is beginning now. I'm sure of it," and he looked as if he could believe it.

Ilona, coming in with the mink coat, swung it wide, ready to fling it all over the covers.

"Ilona," her father said.

Startled by this mild rebuke, she turned. "What?"

"Not your mother's coat. Handling it like that."

"My God," she whispered, aghast. Then she cried angrily, "Don't be so silly," and flung the mink coat over the other coats. While Ilona bent over her mother, stroking her hair, Dubuque couldn't bear to look at Mr. Tomory. Ilona's words, "Don't be so silly," and the stricken expression that had come on her father's face made Dubuque so uncomfortable he wanted to get out of the house. Was Mr. Tomory still trying to pretend that everything was normal, he wondered; and did he believe they could prove it by carrying on as they always did in their house, carrying on with dignified respect for the special things that had secret importance for them? But Mrs. Tomory, startling them, whispered, "Oh, that feels so good. Thank you, Ilona."

Turning to smile at Mr. Tomory, Dubuque could tell by the bewildered expression on the man's face that something that had been real for him and Ilona was no longer real. But then he heard the sound of the ambulance siren on the street.

"Here it is," he said, and running down the stairs, he opened the door and stood on the veranda, waving his arms. It was snowing harder now, but the air felt mild and good. The ambulance attendants, carrying a stretcher with red blankets, came running into the house. "Upstairs," Dubuque said. "I think she's had some kind of hemorrhage . . . the stomach, maybe. I don't know." Leaving the stretcher at the foot of the stairs after setting it up, the two white-coated attendants went up the stairs, carrying blankets. Dubuque waited at the foot of the stairs. Finally they came down, one of them backing down the stairs carrying Mrs. Tomory, and followed by Mr. Tomory, who was putting on his overcoat, and Ilona, who now had on one of the cloth coats that had been on the bed. "Okay?" one of the attendants asked. "Okay," the other replied, and they took Mrs. Tomory out to the ambulance.

In the hall, where Ilona and Mr. Tomory were buttoning their coats in silence—uneasy with each other in this silence—Dubuque again felt uncomfortable. His fur hat was in the living room, and he went in to get it. Then he turned and looked back at the room with its rich rug and antiques. He looked at that one fat lighted red candle and felt upset. Ilona and her father had said nothing to each other as they stood there. And the living room now looked very empty.

Outside, locking the door, Mr. Tomory said with dignity, "Thank you very much, Mr. Dubuque. You are very kind." But Ilona, following the stretcher, got into the ambulance and waited for her father. Before the ambulance door was closed Dubuque called, "Ilona—let me know how it goes. Right?" She waved to him and said something, but the ambulance door had closed. With a wail of its siren and its red light flashing, the ambulance went along the street in the thick-falling snow. A lot of little red lights gleamed in windows of houses along the street and the big flashing red ambulance light in the snow was supported in its fiery glow by these other little lights. While Dubuque stood in the snow, flakes melting at the back of his neck, the ambulance light vanished around the corner.

When he did not hear from Ilona the next day, he felt hurt. But he told himself that, after all, he was not an old family friend, and she would have other things on her mind at this time. But when he telephoned the To-mory house the next day and no one answered, he be-came alarmed, though he tried to believe that Ilona and her father would be at the hospital. On the fourth night he drove to the Tomory house. When no one answered his knock, he went next door. A plump, pleasant-faced young woman came to the door. "I'm a friend of the Tomorys," he said. "I've been trying to get in touch with them. No one answers the phone. Aren't they around at all?"

"Mr. Tomory has been in and out,". the young woman said. Then, hesitating, "Didn't you know that Mrs. Tomory died?"

"She died?"

"The night they took her to the hospital. We saw the ambulance in the snow. When you see an ambulance come next door you try to find out what happened, okay? Mr. Tomory said it was a massive stomach hemorrhage. I think they opened her up. God knows what they found. Did you know she was sick?"

"I knew," he said.

"I'm sorry about it," she said. "They were good neighbors. A little odd. Kept very much to themselves and satisfied about it. But very polite." The young woman had an honest, open face, and was also very polite.

"What about Miss Tomory?" he asked. "Has Miss Tomory been around?"

"Miss Tomory? I don't know her at all. I mean, I know her just to see her. The Tomorys—I believe he said they have a relative here, and Mr. Tomory, with his wife dead, was staying with this relative. Miss Tomory? Come to think of it, I saw her come here yesterday with a man, and leave with him."

"A big man? Black hair? Well dressed?"

"That's the one."

"Thank you," he said.

"Watch the ice on the step," she said.

19

AROUND THE BRADLEY THEY HAD COME TO BELIEVE they would never see Ilona again, for no one had any information about her, and Dubuque now seldom came into the lounge. When he did, he never went into Mr. Gilhooley's. The girls on "the block" had begun to tell stories about Ilona, stories that got passed around among their clients. Ellie, on the block, liked telling about the night when she and Daphne and Joyce cornered Ilona on the lot across the street, ready to beat her up, and how she had awed them just with her presence and her air of lofty command. Ellie said, "Then I knew it must be true she was a real Hungarian princess," and when the client said, "There are no Hungarian princesses," Ellie answered, "How do I know? Maybe a countess then. She had to be one or the other." The regulars in the lounge who had seen her at her table, or had even approached her, told stories about sleeping with her and discovering that, being rich, she wouldn't take any money. According to them she also had fantastically alluring little tricks in bed. Rich and high-born, she could do what she wanted to do, they said. It was as if those who had seen her at work in the lounge had to keep changing the story a little, changing it till they got it in the right shape.

"Who the hell is this woman they're talking about?" Dubuque asked whenever he heard one of these exasperating stories. He had decided once and for all to put Ilona out of his mind. He had no hold on her; she had taken up a lot of his time, he hadn't made a nickel, and she couldn't do him any good. Yet one night just before going out for dinner with his wife, he suddenly grabbed the telephone book, looked up the number of Rupert Sills's residence, and called. When he got a young woman with an attractive voice he asked importantly for Rupert Sills himself. Mr. Sills was not at home, she said; was there anything she could do? She was Mrs. Sills. "Well, possibly, just possibly," he said, trying to sound like a man of learning. "My name is Edmund J. Dubuque and Johnny Sills lent me some money months ago. I'd like to pay him back. I've tried the university. . . ."

"My goodness, you must be a rare and interesting fellow," she said, laughing, "trying to find a man to give him some money." Johnny was out of town, she said. But when he came home she would certainly give him the message. Dubuque could almost see her broad smile and, liking her tone, he thought he might do business with that one some day. He was satisfied that Johnny, having made peace with his family, now had some money, and could afford a trip that would delight Ilona. Putting her out of his mind for good this time, he thought, he went out to dinner with his wife.

She was soon to give him a son, and every time he looked at her he felt proud, grateful, and anxious to please her. Taking her on a trip to New York he encouraged her to spend his money. When they came home the city was snowbound after a March blizzard. This city had little or no spring: ice and snow, then warm summer sunlight. The sudden thaw flooded the street crossings, and there was a blue sky and mild air.

One Saturday afternoon, in this fine weather, Dubuque was in a downtown department store buying some bath salts for his wife. He saw a vaguely familiar figure about thirty feet away at a counter in the book department. He couldn't be sure, because he could only see the head and shoulders. Watching, he waited. The middle-aged man with the black fedora and dark grey overcoat moved slowly around the table loaded with books being remaindered by a publisher. When Dubuque's purchase had been parcelled, he approached the book counter. "Why, Mr. Tomory," he said, putting out his hand.

"Mr. Dubuque. Ah, this is a very good thing."

"I tried to get in touch with you, Mr. Tomory. Look, I was sorry about your wife."

"Thank you. I remember how very helpful you were, Mr. Dubuque."

"It was a tough one. A real tough one. I had no luck getting in touch with you."

"I wasn't at home very much. No," and he sighed. "It was not a good time to be at home alone." He still had his gracious little smile. He was still comforting himself with his natural dignity, yet without any of that amused philosophic grace he had shown while talking about being a reader of gas meters, throwing the beam of his flashlight in the dark cellars of the world.

"How are those gas meters?" Dubuque asked, to lighten the conversation.

"Well, it's a job," he said, shrugging.

"Yeah, so it is," Dubuque said, regretting that he had mentioned the job, and with an effort at casual ease he asked, "What do you hear from Ilona?"

"Oh, I do hear from her, Mr. Dubuque."

"That's great."

"At first I didn't hear," he said, as if Dubuque would understand why he was half apologetic. "Since then I've had some fine letters."

"That is good news. Where is she?"

"In Mexico. A village outside Mexico City. By this time she may be married. Have you met the man? You have? He came around just once that day after her mother's funeral. I wish I knew him better. I liked him. I could talk to him. But off they went. You see, her mother's death seemed to . . . well, things that were there at home aren't there now. Maybe it's better for Ilona. Well, her man Johnny's an intellectual. A seeker. Maybe he's lucky he can afford it. All very interesting to me. Ilona loves writing letters. We have relatives in Montreal. She used to write a lot to her cousin there. Lovely letters."

"And she told you what's going on? And how it is with her?"

"She knows how I like all the little details."

"About what's going on around her?"

"Exactly."

"Look, Mr. Tomory, there's a coffee shop here. Will you have a coffee with me? I'd love to hear what she's doing."

"Why, yes, I'd like a coffee," he said. And they went down to the coffee shop. When they were sitting side by side at the counter, sipping their coffee, Dubuque said, "Why Mexico? Why did they go to Mexico?"

"At first it was just a happy idea, she tells me. But Johnny is a university man. He had a friend, a musician, who shared his interests at the American university in Mexico City."

Mr. Tomory must have been wanting to talk to someone about Ilona, tell about her as he would have told it to his wife if she had been ill and unable to read the letter. In the beginning the trip to Mexico had evidently been a lark, he said. Johnny was at loose ends and a drunk. But with Ilona at his side, he took hold of himself. His musician friend at the university told him about a great teacher from Asia who had come to America.

While Mr. Tomory talked on and on, Dubuque did not interrupt him. He let him finish his coffee, and got him another cup. "But you say she didn't stay in Mexico City," he said. "Didn't she like the place?"

"She loved it, Mr. Dubuque. They stopped for a while at an expensive hotel, and she had everything, and the great boulevards reminded Johnny of Paris. It is a pink city, she said. Not the buildings, just the light, and she saw the beggars, the poverty, the little Indian kids on the street corners in this soft light, but Johnny was serious now about his studies and he took a cottage thirty miles away from Mexico City where he could work. Ever hear of a place called Boulder, Mr. Dubuque?"

"Never heard of it."

"It's in Colorado. A university there. A big school for meditation, and this Asian teacher was visiting there. Well, Johnny wrote to this teacher wanting to become one of his students. He didn't get an answer. So with Ilona he flew all the way to Boulder, and imagine this: the professor wouldn't see him."

"Why not?"

"Who knows? Sounds like strange stuff, doesn't it, Mr. Dubuque?"

"Holy Moses. Him there with Ilona."

"Yes, Ilona says she felt out of place. The women nice, but all dowdy, and she and Johnny went back to Mexico and he's there now. Disciplining himself, she says. Training his spirit and trying to keep in touch with the great teacher at Boulder. The thing is, Mr. Dubuque, she's happy living with Johnny deep in that country."

"Does it make any sense to you, Mr. Tomory?" Dubuque asked.

"I only know this," he said. "I can tell by the way she writes she's happy with this other world opening up to her. I like to think of her there, with this happening, Mr. Dubuque," he said, his head back, and with a dreamy smile, nodding, his eyes full of faraway places. "I like thinking of her in a particular place she wrote about. It is a place about forty miles outside Mexico City, a place, she said, which is really a great avenue of ancient pyramids. I like seeing her walking on this vast avenue in that pinkish light under that wild Mexican sky, Johnny Sills with his arm around her, telling her about the religion of those ancient people—Ilona in that great old world. Yes, I can see her—" His pleased and dreamy expression, finally broken by a little laugh, left Dubuque bemused. He felt as he had on that night leaving their family home, imagining he had left some hidden antique theatre.

"Would you have another coffee?" he asked, smiling.

"No, no, I must go, Mr. Dubuque."

"It must have been quite a letter."

"Yes, she writes a beautiful letter."

As they left the coffee shop, Dubuque said, "Look if you write to her, remember me to her, eh?"

"Indeed, I will, Mr. Dubuque."

"Tell her I think about her a lot."

"I will, Mr. Dubuque."

"Ask her if she'll write me a good letter just to tell me how things worked out for her. And you? Are you living alone?"

"Living alone is no good," he said, sighing. "Our place—what we put into it—living there together, we put a lot into it. Yes, with some pride in the way we lived with each other. Well, I have a relative in Vancouver. I need people of my own I like. The relative I have here, I don't really like. Too busy."

"You don't mean you're thinking of moving to Vancouver?"

"That's just what I'm thinking of doing. In fact, if I can sell the house . . ." and he smiled. "Do you want to buy a house?"

"You'll have no trouble. Not these days."

"That's right. No trouble. A dealer is coming to look at the furniture."

"He is, eh? Well—those guys . . ." Dubuque began, holding Mr. Tomory with his eyes while he wondered what was going on in the back of his own mind. "Some of those things I liked a lot," he said. "Look, Mr. Tomory," then he hesitated, liking what he suddenly saw in his mind's eye. "My own office is more like a sitting room than a business office. It's the way I do business. Do you know something? I can see that Chinese rug in my office. I can see a couple of those chairs with it. Yeah, Mr. Tomory, if you're really clearing out the stuff, will you promise to let me know?"

"A pleasure, Mr. Dubuque."

"Here's my card. The telephone number is on it."

"You may hear from me. Why not, Mr. Dubuque?"

"Yes, why not, and good luck, Mr. Tomory," and they parted.

Two weeks later he got a call from Mr. Tomory, who said he had sold his house and if Mr. Dubuque wanted to make an offer for any of the furnishings he would be glad to entertain it before calling in the antique dealer. "I'll come to your house at once," Dubuque said, and he went to the house and paid a thousand dollars for the rug and five hundred for the two fine carved-oak chairs. At the last moment, as if something had suddenly amused him, he asked, "By the way, what about that old mink coat Ilona used to wear? For me, you know—a keepsake. Or maybe I could have it made into a jacket for my wife." Astonished, Mr. Tomory said, "My wife's coat? Oh, you wouldn't want it, it's been fixed so often, just to make it look good. No wonder Ilona left it behind. I don't know why she wasted her money having a new lining put in it." But needing the money as he did, and admitting that the coat still looked good, he took a hundred dollars.

Two days later, after the Chinese rug had been laid in his office and the two antique chairs had replaced his big red leather one, Dubuque sat at his desk, his hands linked behind his neck. He assured himself that the furnishings had been a great buy and he couldn't lose a nickel on the deal because they gave the office a certain tone that made him seem to be an established figure. And as for the coat, the great long coat now hanging on the oak coat-tree with the seven prongs near the door— anyone coming into the office and seeing the coat would imagine an expensive woman was close at hand; a good impression to make on any man. While he was ruminating in this way the door opened and Gil came in.

"Gil," he said, startled. "Well, long time no see."

"Yeah, where have you been? I've been wanting to talk to you."

"Sure, I know," Dubuque said warily.

"Oh, who told you?" Gil said, looking around the office. He stared at the coat. When he sat down in one of the antique chairs, his face was full of surprise. "Your office, Jay? It doesn't look like you."

"Well, it's me. What's on your mind?"

"Can you come out? I want to buy you a drink. You see, there's stuff you know—stuff I don't know."

"About what?"

"Ilona. I don't even know where she is."

"Well, she's in Mexico."

"Mexico? Are you sure? How do you know?"

"Her father. Ran into him in a department store."

"What's she doing in Mexico?"

"Doing it with that goddamn Sills, and apparently, at least according to the old man, doing all right. Why not? They'll have the Sills money. Come on now, Gil. What are you up to? What's the point?"

"Okay. Now look, Jay, you know something about me. You know I have a bar, yes. And I'm comfortable. Yes," Gil said. "But this you don't know. I'm a writer. I've been all over the continent, making money, but I always told myself I would go on being a writer and would get to work and prove it again when the right story took hold of me." A flush had come on his cheeks. He was embarrassed to be revealing himself candidly to Dubuque.

Laughing, he tried to be humorous about it. Many a man, being one thing, tries to kid himself, tries to keep some dream he had of himself when younger, he said. In Chicago, in Vegas, in New Orleans, he had met characters he could see were wonderfully colorful and entertaining, and he had thought he would write about them. But he hadn't, because, he supposed, not one of them had made him keep saying to himself, "I want to know this about her, or that about him. I want to know why." And this was the way it was now with Ilona.

"Why the hell are you telling this to me?" Dubuque asked. In all the years they had known each other, Gil had never granted him a moment of real intimacy.

"Because you're the one who knows about Ilona," Gil said.

"Oh, we all know about Ilona, don't we?"

"You know more. There's stuff you can tell me." With a sudden respect and even a warmth in his eye as if he wanted to draw close, he said, "You're in the story, Jay."

"Oh. As what?"

"I don't know yet. But there. Mysteriously there."

"Such big words. A story, eh? A book?"

"I know it'll get told."

"You got a contract?"

"I don't care about that. I have to go on with it. I really have to. Do you know she's already becoming a legend around that hotel?"

"Around a hotel," Dubuque said sourly.

"Come on, can we have a drink? Can we talk?"

"Yeah. We can talk," Dubuque said, getting up.

When they were at the door Dubuque stopped and, patting the mink coat on the tree, he said, "She won't stay with Johnny Sills, you know, because she's a natural-born hooker. She has to leave him, and she will leave him. Well, I've done a little thinking about her and this rare thing she has. Yeah, I figured it out It's intimacy, Gil. The world is full of lonely people. And this is why—no real intimacy. It must be that Ilona creates the illusion of intimacy. It must be just an illusion, right? Hell, how do I know?"

While Gil waited, watching intently, growing more fascinated, Dubuque went on. "She talked to me about a famous old French fashion figure in her eighties who said if she had it to do over again she might like to have been a famous courtesan. Ilona—" and turning on Gil he said scornfully—"a legend around a little hotel, you say? Hell, Ilona could have become a real legend. . . . Well, come on. Let's have a drink."

20

THEN FOR A WEEK DUBUQUE WAS BUSY DOING A profitable collection job for Manny Gerber, who ran a big floating crap game. An almost disbarred lawyer with a mania for gambling who owed Manny Gerber a hundred thousand dollars had made it clear that payment of the debt was going to take a long, long time. He knew he couldn't be sued, and anyway, his big house and everything else he owned were now in his wife's name. When Gerber offered Dubuque twenty per cent of what he could collect, Dubuque put two of his men, Big Red and Fat Morris, to work. The lawyer's car was burned, all the front of his house was painted red with spray guns, the dock of his country cottage was set afire. And so by the end of the week Manny Gerber received a large payment from the lawyer, with the promise of more to come when the house was mortgaged. A fat cheque came to Dubuque. It had been a very good week, and at the end of the week he received a letter from Ilona. She wrote:

My father tells me that he talked to you. You often think about me, he said, and he told me that you had bought the rug and some of our chairs for your office. Nor do I forget how you tried to be of help with my mother. So I felt I owe it to you to let you know how it has been with me. This then is to be a good long letter.

It is night. I'm alone in our cottage in the hills. It is a quaint little adobe house with a garden full of heavy splashy flowers everywhere, and strange trees, and at night so black and lonely I'm afraid to walk out alone. Tonight, as I write, it is raining. I write to you because I know now—I feel it in my bones—that you are still looking around for me and waiting. Here at night, when I'm alone and it's black and raining, I can feel you waiting. And I know that being the kind of man you are, you'll go on waiting till you are convinced that I am no longer in your world. Well, Johnny Sills has taken me into his own life, into his dreams, into his work, into places you could never know. Johnny, who's so big, dark, and impulsive with so much wild restlessness in him, shows a marvellous respect for me, and unlike some big strong men he has the courage to be gentle, sensually gentle, touching the flesh on my arms, just pressing the flesh with his finger, making it something special, and his passion for me in bed—a real hunger, and then afterwards, lying beside me, finding such peace within himself.

He talks to me—my God, it's wonderful to have a man wanting me to know everything about himself. And he tells me about his father, the top dollar man in a city full of top dollar men. And the strange thing is that when we're together, looking around at the village people, I see everything in a good light. He says he knows he can't be a poet, but he can try to be an artist about his own life, which, I suppose, doesn't mean much to you, Dubuque, but when I listen to him, talking about giving a shape to his life, I think of my parents' home, and my mother in her antique Chinese pyjamas. It's not your world, Dubuque. It's far away from you. It's a world I love now, a world where you could never be. You will believe me, I know, when you really understand that I am happy and satisfied.

Johnny had been away for a week at a place called Boulder in Colorado and she had been alone in the house, she wrote. A sixteen-year-old Mexican boy from a family that lived down the road was paid to watch over her, and the house, and the boy with his big dog practically sleeping on the doorstep, seemed to belong with the heavy green trees, the sunlight, and the garden with the crazy flowers, she wrote. She liked being by herself, as she was now, writing this long letter, because she never felt alone, waiting for the one man who needed her. She was living with this man, she wrote, and she wanted him, Dubuque, to know what excitement and happiness she found just waiting for Johnny.

When Dubuque had finished reading the letter he fell into a long reverie. Then, after looking at his watch—it was just before noontime—he put the letter in his pocket, left the office, and headed for Mr. Gilhooley's. At this time the bar was deserted and would be for another half-hour. "Don't look so surprised, Gil," he said. "I've heard from our lady—from Mexico. I thought you'd like to read the letter. Here it is."

He watched the changing expressions on Gil's face as he read, the growing pleasure, the final satisfaction. Handing the letter back, smiling, Gil said, "Another great thing is that the lady writes like a lady."

"Sounds just like herself to me."

"Anyway, she's made it."

"Made it where?"

"Well—to the other shore—if you know what I mean."

"You can really see her—far off somewhere?"

"I can, I surely can."

"Well, I can't. No. I see her in the snow. Always in the snow. The snow's all gone now, but it'll be back as she'll be back, Gil. Yeah, I know she will. It's like those people who think they'll drive a taxi just for a while to get some money to go on with something else. They always come back to it. Haven't you noticed?"

21

SPRING HAD COME SO SLOWLY THAT THE WHITE-
painted Bradley House in the new bright sunlight bore
all the scars of the lingering winter. The soot-laden
snows had smudged the white walls. Mr. Bradley, who
had returned from Florida with the twins, had immediately ordered the spring clean-up. High-pressure hoses
had been scouring the brick, washing the walls down,
and now the hotel shone as brightly in the new sunlight
as it did at night-time under its own floodlights.

Mr. Bradley was bent on having his Saturday suppers again, and at the first one of these dinners he had his
regulars: Judge Gibbons, the Irish television producer
who wore the leather cap which he still kept on at the
table, and Gil, and, of course, the twins, now sun-tanned
and elegant in new summer dresses. Mr. Bradley, his leg
brace discarded, looked older after his long vacation in
the sun; his face, too, was more flushed.

But it was a good jovial dinner. The Judge was the

judge of old. That girl he had jailed because she wouldn't testify against her lover he had suddenly freed. Things at home had changed for him, too. He had rediscovered the melancholy poetry of A. E. Housman, and at dinner he did a little reciting. "An Englishman turned Greek," he said, "but of course, the Greeks were never melancholy."

Suddenly interrupting the Judge, Bradley said, "I've heard a story—I've heard more or less the same story from business friends who don't know our lounge, yet know this story. It's about a rich young aristocratic woman, long mink coat and all, who came to our lounge three or four times a week, and played whore. Did you ever see her there, Gil? Is there any truth in that story?"

"Some truth, yes," Gil said. "She didn't come into the bar. I used to catch a glimpse of her through the grill. Yeah, she was there."

"I saw her too," the Judge said calmly.

"You saw her?"

"I'm sure I did," the Judge said, smiling. "Sitting at the bar talking to Gil, I turned, looked through that lattice, and saw this lovely, elegant woman at her table. Very rich, you say. Why do you say she was rich?"

Before Bradley could answer, Ellen said, "What a kinky way for a rich girl to get her kicks. How did the other girls let her get away with it? That's what I'd like to know."

But Bradley, cutting Ellen off, said he also had heard the lady was a Hungarian countess, and now no one knew where she had gone, but some men still came to the hotel, really believing she would show up again. "It's a good story, anyway," he said. "The more often this story is told, the more often people will want to come to the lounge just to ask about her. I like it."

While Bradley talked, the Judge, holding Gil's eyes,

kept smiling and Gil, nodding, smiled too. And in the exchange of glances, and their silence, they were sharing a liking and a truth about each other.

More often than he used to, the Judge came to Mr. Gilhooley's, and when he did the night never passed without his mentioning Ilona, but just casually, as if she were someone they knew so well, her name could come up in any conversation. The Judge told Gil that he had reclaimed his dog, Bruno, from the friend in the country. And now, just as he used to do, he walked Bruno at midnight, and just as he used to, he pushed his wife's wheelchair around the neighborhood, the dog walking with them. His wife, who was really a wise woman, the Judge said, had known when she came home from the hospital and found the dog in the house that she had lost her domination, and said nothing.

Sometimes Gil and the Judge talked about Ilona being in Mexico, talking about her as if she were someone who had gone so far away they could never know anything more about her. And Gil kept storing up stories Bradley told at his dinner table, stories about the rich woman, the countess who had suddenly vanished. As the stories changed, Gil became certain that no one, not even Dubuque, had really known her, and in his imagination she kept taking on a larger life and different forms. He wondered if all this stuff now came out of his own fancy. When he got confused in his story-telling, he would remember the night at his parents' home and how he had brought the news of his brother's death and told about the girl he had loved; and how his heart-broken mother, her eyes lighting up, had whispered, "Why, it's a story." Though he knew that it could never possibly be, he was sure that if his mother could have known Ilona she would understand what he meant when he talked to her about that woman in his brother's life.

As the weeks passed they stopped talking about Ilona. Not that she had been forgotten. No, she had settled in; she was there to be remembered at any time—available to be remembered. At his Saturday dinners, Mr. Bradley no longer asked questions about her. After one of these dinners Gil returned to his bar, where the Saturday-night regulars expected him to be for the rest of the evening, and Hazel, seeing him come in, waved and beckoned eagerly. But not until he had put on his little black coat did he go to her.

"Our lady's back," she said.

"Our lady?"

"Ilona."

"No!"

"See for yourself." And he looked through the lattice.

There she was at the table where she used to sit, wearing a suede jacket, her head at the old superior angle, the same fine features, but the face—now it was another face, and Gil felt heavy, dull, and leaden with disappointment.

"When did she come in?" he asked Hazel.

"A couple of hours ago."

"And the girls on the block?"

"No one wants her around here, Gil."

"No one, yeah. No one," Gil said. Then he thought of Dubuque, though it hurt to think of him. It was a terrible thing that he needed the company of Dubuque now, rather than a man like Judge Gibbons. He got to the telephone and called the Dubuque house. He called four times before Dubuque answered, listened, and made no comment other than to say he would come right around.

22

UNAWARE THAT ILONA WAS AT HER TABLE ON THE other side of the grill, a little group had gathered around Melissa Macey, a handsome actress with a bold mouth, who, perched on her bar stool, held court telling of her trip to Athens and her meeting with Melina Mercouri. Melissa had a sharp tongue and a remarkable gift for the lingo and got bursts of laughter. But Gil knew that soon these people would hear that Ilona, the rich countess, as they had it now, had returned; soon they would want to gape at her; soon word would spread around the neighborhood. Maybe even Bradley himself would come down to have a look, maybe the twins, too, would want to see for themselves. Yet the girls on the block, as disappointed as he was himself, would go on scowling at her.

Standing beside Gil and upset by his troubled eyes and fixed smile, Hazel whispered cynically, "It's just a local event, Gil. It isn't as if the nuclear war has begun. Just the same, what I can't figure out is those other little whores. I heard that girl, Ellie . . . Well, you'd really have a story if they turned on Ilona and tore her to pieces. I can't figure them out. . . ."

"I think I can," Gil whispered. But then he saw Dubuque. "Excuse me, Hazel," he said.

Though Dubuque was grim-eyed and grim of mood, it wasn't because of the news of Ilona's return. The three bookies who had wanted to remain independent of his organization had brought in Willie the Weeper, the well-known enforcer from Montreal. But Dubuque, getting wind of this, had had Willie met at the airport, and looked after. Lying in a farmer's barn out near the airport, his legs broken, sobbing in pain, Willie had screamed after Dubuque, walking out of the barn, "You're a dead man, Dubuque. My brothers'll get you. They'll come here, and you're dead." The screaming threats, following Dubuque, made him turn though he was ten feet away from the barn door, and he went limping slowly back. A broad shaft of late-afternoon sunlight coming through the wide-open doors shone on the Weeper's face and on his shattered legs. He was clutching a handful of straw from the barn floor. As Dubuque stood over him saying nothing there was a long silence, and then the Weeper's eyes, so bright in that shaft of sunlight, in that silence, grew wide with terror. He whispered, "Please—no—" and Dubuque, holding the silence a little longer, then turned away and walked out into the sunlight and not even a moan now came from the barn.

Trying to get away from the unpleasant experience, Dubuque had changed his clothes, and had taken off the three-piece executive suit. He now wore an Irish tweed hat, a camel's-hair jacket, and black slacks; a man of the establishment, dressed for the relaxing weekend. Beckoning to Gil to come away from Melissa's flow of vigorous language and the accompanying laughter, he said quietly, "I told you she couldn't stay with Johnny Sills, didn't I?"

"I know you did," Gil said.

"Or anybody else?"

"I know. But good God—just the same . . ."

"Well, where is she?"

"Look in there." Disappointed by Dubuque's composure, Gil watched him go to the grill and peer into the lounge, standing there a long time, saying nothing. Finally Dubuque said, "The dew is off the grass, yeah—well . . ." After ruminating, his head down, he suddenly banged open the swing door, the first such push given that door by anyone since the last time he himself had used it, and entered the lounge.

Approaching Ilona's table, he held back. A stocky, solemn, red-haired fellow who had been eying her intently from his place four tables away was about to sit down with her. She appraised him shrewdly. Their heads came together in earnest negotiation, just all hard business. She looked more frigidly superior—the face lines, the set of her head, made her seem a woman born to look down her nose. A grim little satisfied twist had come to the red-haired man's mouth, as if he could see himself on the bed with her, and see himself as the one who could shatter forever her cool superiority, making her cry out in pain. Seeing Dubuque taking an anxious step toward her, she dismissed the red-haired man. "Go away," she said, "I'm busy."

Dubuque said, "Well, you're back."

"Yeah, I'm back."

"As I knew you would be."

"Okay. So you're right."

"Just the same, I'm disappointed. No, I'm god-damned disappointed."

"That's a switch, isn't it? What's got into you?"

"I got that letter. The world was your oyster. What happened?"

"After I wrote the letter?" Her smile too bright, too hard, she said, "What do you want? That I should go on with the letter?"

"Tell me why you left him."

"Well, I couldn't go on with him."

"Oh? Go on where?"

"On a journey."

"A journey. A journey where?" But over by the entrance an altercation was taking place. A middle-aged, pale-faced man with dark glasses had been refused entrance to the lounge and now was struggling with the bouncer, who had twisted his arm high up his back. Dubuque thought that Ilona, who had turned, was watching intently. Then he saw that other things, other places, were in her eyes. "To the East," she said solemnly. "The sun rises in the east, doesn't it?" Then, catching herself, or hurt by the sound of her own voice, she changed, laughing again, too brightly. In a lazy drawl she said, "Yes, I suppose I should have gone with him. I'd like to see the East. Cathay, they call it Cathay, don't they? To ride an elephant, shoot a tiger, get lost for a day in a swarm of people in Calcutta." But she had begun to fumble her words. It was the first time he had ever seen her keyed up and breathing hard, trying to hold back. Yet she went on, "I brought something, the only thing I wanted to bring back. Not silver bracelets and earrings and stuff. A little wooden carving about eight inches wide. Two clasped hands, just two hands cut off at the wrists. If you really liked it I might give it to you. I got it from one of those little Indian shops by the roadside in Mexico City." Her eyes now were dreamy. "This old Indian had all kinds of stuff, masks and carvings and bracelets. Then I saw this carving, just the two clasped hands cut off at the wrists."

Her words sounded so out of place here that Dubuque looked around uncomfortably. The new girl on the block, Dusky, was rebuffing a client she hated, and coming into the lounge was a huge, two-hundred-and-fifty-pound blonde woman with a big, self-satisfied smile, accompanied by two serious-faced skinny men.

"Ilona," Dubuque said, "in that letter you said you were full of happiness, waiting for Johnny to return. Go on from there."

But her eyes, shifting away from him, grew fixed on the big wide mirror over the bar which reflected all the lounge lights, the colored walls, the bottles, and the shifting, changing faces in depths of shadow, then in gleaming light, all holding her hypnotically as if she now could see herself in that cottage room at night, writing the letter. "Yeah," she said finally, "I should have waited till he returned. As soon as I saw him I knew he had had no luck. The great director had refused to see him, and worse still, he had not been permitted to attend the lectures. Yet after he had sat down opposite me, he began to smile and, well, we went to bed. Doing it with him, well, this is what he had often said, and why it was so easy to remember—he said when he was doing it with me, it was like being caught in a slow, gentle flow of things, then being taken along to a kind of shiver where everything seemed to be there in your hand and shining bright—the one ancient mystery, the core of all mysteries. That was the way he put it, word for word," she said.

She had remained on the bed, she went on, her eyes closed, all spent, and he had got a dressing gown to throw over her, because it was surprisingly cool at night. When he didn't cover her, she opened her eyes; he was looking down at her thighs, meditating, almost in a trance.

She was distracted by a commotion in the lounge, following the wail of a siren. It was the sound of a fire engine coming close to the hotel, and stopping, then the sound of another siren, another engine coming close. Some patrons in the lounge, getting up, headed for the entrance. A man at the door called, "Just a blaze in that cleaning and pressing shop." Dubuque had stood up, but Ilona hadn't moved. In her mind she was still in that Mexican bedroom with Johnny bending over her naked body.

"Go on," Dubuque said, sitting down.

After that night she noticed a change in him, she went on. His respect for her was almost reverential, yet she couldn't get him to come to bed with her. He kept going into Mexico City to have conferences with his religious friends. "When he returned, he found the will to leave me untouched," she said, "and I said to myself, 'He's found another girl,' but I couldn't believe it, because his eyes lit up when he met me. He has beautiful deep-set eyes, you know. When I put my arms around him, wanting him, I could feel him hard with wanting me. It was really fascinating, you know," she said. Her head was on one side, and Dubuque waited, watching the shadows on her face.

Then she said, "I remember lying on the bed listening to night sounds outside the window, like night birds calling and little animals rustling around, and I remember glancing at Johnny, who had put down the book he was reading and was watching me. Well, when a woman is lying half naked on a bed and finds a man watching her intently, just watching and wondering, she feels lonely and far away from him, and I asked, 'Johnny, what is it about me?' And he said, 'I think it's the promise in you,' and I said, 'Promise of what?' and he said, 'Things that used to seem beyond me. Oh, I don't know. Forget it.' Then I said, 'Johnny, sooner or later won't we have to go home?'

"And when he just looked at me, I remembered that he had never asked questions about my life at home, and I remembered, too, that when I had tried to tell him about Robert he hadn't been interested, he hadn't listened. You'd think he'd want to know things about me, old things, wouldn't you? My school days. 'Oh, who cares about school days,' he said, and when I tried to tell him about the first time I took money from a man—no interest at all. Even irritation. Why was he so afraid of learning anything about my life? Were we there in Mexico because, from the beginning, we had to get a thousand miles away from his home and my home and the life I had led at home? Did I exist for him only when we were far away from home?

"Well, listen to this. A letter came from his musician friend, and that did it. In this letter Johnny was told he was to go to an ashram in Hawaii, where there was an important teacher who would welcome him, and he could continue his studies with the teacher, and though it meant he would be leaving me, he looked excited and happy. Imagine! And him sitting there smiling at me! I grabbed his head, jerking it hard to make him listen, and asked why he and his saintly friends were all so god-damned self-centred and ruthless, and weren't they lucky they had the money to humor themselves, and I cried,

'Oh, Johnny, why can't you ever see what's right under your nose?'

"And this is what he answered," she went on. "I can tell you exactly because I wrote it down so I would remember it. He said, 'Ilona, for one kind of man . . . well, it's all in that poem, do you know it? "A primrose by the river's brim a yellow primrose was to him—and nothing more." I'm not that kind of a man,' and I yelled, 'What the hell's the matter with a beautiful primrose? You may know a lot about that big inner world of yours, but you don't realize the wonder of things around you,' and I startled him, I guess, and he cried, 'Hey, what is this?' and I said, 'I don't care about all this lofty mystical nonsense. The fact is you don't want to know anything about me. For God's sake, what are you afraid of?' and he said, 'I know how much I needed you, I know.' And I said, 'That's all right. But the fact is you don't want to know anything about me.'"

Pausing a moment, she eyed Dubuque, waiting, tense and challenging, and he did not know what hard comment she expected from him. Shrugging, she said, "Okay, I told him I didn't want a crazy monk, who looked at a woman just to try and see beyond her. I told him I had a life as a woman. I told him I had my own dreams. I told him I was a woman with a life quite apart from his—with my own loneliness and my hope he might at least come brushing against me. I told him I wouldn't go on being the goddamned object that set off his sexual fantasies—crazy dreams of stuff beyond him and me, and where we were, I had had enough of it. I was no stepping-stone. And he shouted at me, 'I know what you're trying to do. You're trying to get me to go home and settle into a life,' and I said, 'A real life, yeah, Johnny, but you're afraid. You're afraid to learn that I am what I am, and there's nothing more. And that's as it should be, nothing more. You're blind as a bat, Johnny, so to hell with you, and I won't miss you.'

"Oh, by the way, Jay," she broke off, brightening. "The morning we were to go into the city I happened to look out the window and saw those big heavy strange flowers. Flowers! And suddenly there I was wondering about those red roses you sent my mother. Remember? And I was wondering how you knew red ones would be right for her, though I liked yellow ones."

"I don't know," he said. "Some things just come to me."

Her tone hardening, she said, "Johnny had to give me some money. He's very generous, and so without telling him anything, without even saying good-bye, I got on a plane. And so—"

"Well, well, well," he said after a long reflection. "These soul suckers. 'How can I feel bigger?' That's their only question. Well, let me tell you something, Ilona," he began, sounding objective and presidential. "Let me draw on a little wisdom I picked up in my own life. It's a mistake to give all of yourself to anyone or anything. If you do, what is there to fall back on? You've got to leave something that lets you remain in the driver's seat."

Not a muscle in her face changed as she eyed him, so he went on, "Look, I've got a hunch. I go by my hunches, and I see a little time passing, and I see you looking back, smiling to yourself and feeling sorry for Johnny."

"I had a need of him. A need I had never had."

"Ilona, let me tell you something else." Again leaning closer, again calm, solid, and soothing, he said, "There's a thing in your story you're missing. That guy couldn't take anything good and great away from you, and he knows it, and is settling for trying to remember it. It's your own stuff, Ilona. As for all those guys, about five years pass, then they go into father's business and settle down in houses with many bathrooms. And if they don't, you know what, Ilona? I think they go on trying to remember, and probably have a terrible time dying because at the last moment they see they once had it all in their hands. Yeah, Ilona, I've been around a little myself and I know that no matter how big Johnny gets in the head, the time will come when he'll need what you gave him."

But her expression had changed and kept changing, and he could believe she was wondering if she had been driven back to this place just to hear these things from him. "How is it that you, a criminal, and proud to be such a criminal, can say these things to me?" she asked.

"How is it in Mexico you thought of me?"

"And it turns out you're full of shit. Leave me be, Dubuque."

"That I will," he said, confused now by his own sudden anger. It had been welling up in him, hurting him, and he could no longer control it. "God damn it, you little fool. Well, I should let you have it straight, Ilona. I should let you have it right in the belly. You here now—my God, nothing's beneath you now. No wonder! Look at you—something's gone out of that puss. It went fast, didn't it? I don't like what I see in your face. It's shit I see. Something's gone. Already it's gone. Hell, why am I bothering with you? In a few weeks I wouldn't be found touching you with a ten-foot pole."

But a big-jawed man in a navy-blue suit and white tie had come sauntering over to the table and now said out of the corner of his mouth, "Make up your mind about her, buster, okay?"

"Tomorrow—or the next day, Ilona," Dubuque said awkwardly.

"Thank you, Jay," she said with a dignity that was hurting him painfully when he entered the bar. Gil stood listening to the hilarious group around Melissa. Seeing Dubuque, Gil came to him quickly. "How was she?" he asked. "Did she say why she left Sills?"

"She didn't leave him. He was leaving her."

"No! No, I can't believe it."

"You can't, eh? Well, he's off to the East now chasing some religious rainbows and she'd only be in his way."

"I see," Gil said, his eyes turning inward as if some aspect of it had caught his imagination. "Yeah, I think I see."

"Oh Christ, cut it out. You don't see."

"What are you so mad about?"

"I'm not mad."

"You sound mad."

"I'm trying to make a point."

"What's the point?"

"You don't understand it at all. I know what you want to say, and I've just said it all to her, understand? And she'd say to you what she just said to me. She'd say, 'You're full of shit,' as you are."

"Dubuque, watch your big fat mouth. This is my place."

"I don't care whose place it is."

But Melissa, at the other end of the bar, called, "Gil, I want you to hear this," and Gil left. Turning, Dubuque looked through the grill at Ilona, still at her table with the heavy-jawed big fellow whose companions at the nearby table grinned at her. These three loose-faced men of forty were aware that their friend was feeling bewildered, though at the beginning of his negotiation with Ilona he had been all hard confidence. Gradually, under her inspection, in the presence of her cool condescension, he had tightened up, eying her resentfully as if aware he had become a nobody; and Dubuque thought, when that guy gets her naked on the bed . . .

Dubuque looked at the back of his left hand, the hand on the bar, and the faint scars still on it, and he felt again all the pain of the metal ash tray as Sills crashed it down. And then he remembered later in the alley, holding his belly, staring up at the moon, wanting to get at Sills—still wanting—and Sills safe in Hawaii now, and Ilona—he turned to look at her.

The big man was now alone at the table, but her half-filled glass was still on the table, as was his, and the man was watching the entrance and waiting. Finally he picked up his drink and moved over to the table with his friends. With them he regained his self-importance, his grin. But his mouth became ugly as he talked, his eyes saying, 'Don't worry, I'll handle the lofty bitch in a way she'll never forget.' Then he turned, watching the door impatiently. Scowling, he got up and went out. In a minute he reappeared, then, baffled and angry, turned to the table where he had been with Ilona, drained his glass, drained hers, too, and hurried out.

Watching intently, Dubuque thought, But what if she saw she should get out of here? Why not? Why not?

He left the bar, and outside, looking both ways on the street, he was stirred by the city sounds in the spring night. They made him wonder if it couldn't be that he had found words she had secretly wanted to hear; then he seemed to see her coming into his office in the morning and looking in wonder at the blue Chinese rug with the yellow pattern, and at the chairs, her chairs, then at the coat hanging on the tree, and, maybe for the first time, tears in her eyes.

When he got home his wife was asleep. He did his little routine chores, opening the windows to let the cat out, then carrying out garbage bags to the street, and then, undressing quietly, he got into bed. As always, he disturbed his wife, who, in her half sleep, turned snuggling warmly and voluptuously against him, her arm coming around him, giving him the familiar feeling that all was secure in his own life. Everything indeed was secure.

And yet he couldn't sleep. The downtown night-city noises he had listened to all his life had always helped him to dream himself to sleep. He knew how to do it; mental arithmetic could do it. He dreamt of his money in the bank, adding on the ten-per-cent interest he would get in April, figuring out how he could still be two per cent ahead of the general inflation, and how the house, as Michelle had pointed out, was increasing in value much ahead of inflation and would be the best investment they had made—adding it all up—and then irrelevantly, right out of all this figuring, right out of the dark, there popped into his head a picture of that big, restless, humiliated, brutish man following Ilona.

23

NEXT DAY IN HIS OFFICE HE REMEMBERED HER SAYING, "Thank you," with such dignity, and was sure it meant she intended to come and see him. When she didn't come, he convinced himself that she was waiting to see if he would go looking for her once more, asking herself if now, having had a chance to think it over, he would really be interested in seeking her out again. When she didn't come he suspected that something had happened that prevented her coming, and he got the newspaper and looked for stories about girls being found beaten and strangled in ditches by highways. On the third afternoon there was a heavy downpour, a cloudburst, and later, when the sun came out, suddenly there was a rainbow, and he thought of the white hotel all wet and shining in the sunlight, and on the way home he dropped into Mr. Gilhooley's.

Gil had seen him come in, but had to wait to talk to him. He had to go on listening respectfully to the cabinet minister who until now had always stayed in the car while his driver picked out a girl from the block. "Right, Rodney, right," Gil kept saying.

"And there's all kinds of unemployment," Rodney said.

"Right."

"And with the inflation no one can save any money."

"Right."

"Then how the hell is it there's so much money around? The town is full of money. Your whiskey costs twice as much now. Where do people get the money?"

"They borrow it," Gil said. "Everybody's in debt."

"Right," Rodney said. "So put it on my tab and have one yourself on me," and he left.

Turning to Dubuque, Gil said, "The Rémy Martin, eh?" and then whispered, "Ilona's gone, Jay. She hasn't been back. Hazel talked to Ellie. No one has seen her. No one expects to see her. No one knows where she's gone." Then he broke off, eying Dubuque, wondering how much he should tell him.

Dubuque said, "What are you holding back?"

"Nothing. Nothing at all," Gil said. "Just my own thoughts." And then suddenly, as if he didn't care what Dubuque thought of his twist of fancy, he said, "I'll tell you what I've been thinking. People here know she showed up, okay? They wanted to see the Hungarian aristocrat. The countess, eh? They have heard the stories and weren't sure they could believe them, okay? Now they hear she's shown up again. People saw her. Some can say they saw her, even some who didn't see her."

"What the hell's the point, Gil?"

"I don't care what she told you. I know what's right about it, what I see as true for me. She had vanished, yeah. And there were all the stories, then she shows up and shows it was all real, no matter what they say. And then she vanishes again."

"Gil, my God you can be a fool," Dubuque said sourly. "Look man, you've been around as much as I have. You know what the truth is. The truth is that girl's body will likely be found in some ditch, or hidden in a bush, and found months later. You know this, and you come up with a sentimental line of crap. Hell—sorry," and he walked out.

Leaving the hotel by the side door, as if he did not want Gil to know what he was up to, he limped around the corner and into the lounge, making his way through the tables to the block. Only four girls were there—the others were out with clients. The four, Ellie and Joyce, who were well known to him, and two seventeen-year-old new girls, were engaged in a lively discussion. With the warm weather coming on, Ellie was once again bent on organizing a softball team. "If we can get a sponsor and fancy uniforms and get good, other teams will want to play us," she said, and then became aware of Dubuque leaning over her shoulder. Dubuque made her nervous. Dubuque frightened her. She said respectfully, "Mr. Dubuque, I think you're the only man who could get us a sponsor. If you can't, who can?"

After pondering gravely, he said, "Yeah, I think I could. Why not? I'll have some neighborhood merchants kick in. Give yourself a name. How about 'The Ramblers'? Something like that. Well, see me about it later, Ellie." And then he asked quickly, "Anybody know where Ilona's living?"

"Not me. I didn't speak to her," Ellie said. "I was afraid I'd punch her right on the nose. Wait a minute. I saw Dusky here talking to her. Ain't that right?" and she turned to the new girl, the seventeen-year-old mulatto, who had a velvet skin, a little girl's voice, and crazy eyes. Dusky said that before the other girls agreed no one should talk to her, Ilona had told her she was in a small hotel, the Citadel, five blocks away on Jarvis.

It took Dubuque about ten minutes in his car to get to the Citadel. It was a quiet, respectable-looking old residential hotel, only a few blocks from the apartment house where Johnny Sills had lived. Hookers never used it. The small lounge had old Persian rugs and high-backed old chairs and freshly bleached oak panelling. The man at the desk, bald, grey at the temples, with rimless glasses, had a sternly sedate air.

"Miss Tomory checked out," he said, hardly looking up as he answered.

"You might assist me, sir," Dubuque began. Standing back a little so he would be in full view, he opened his very expensive jacket after tilting back the gentleman's Irish linen hat he now wore, and took a card—Edmund J. Dubuque, Developer—and put it on the desk. "Edmund J. Dubuque," he said. "The truth is I got tied up, sir, and missed the appointment with Miss Tomory. It was important to her career and she'll be disappointed. By any chance did she leave a message for me?"

"She did not, Mr. Dubuque. I'm sorry."

"Then I'll leave a note—an apology. How do I get in touch with her?"

"I have no idea, Mr. Dubuque. She checked out—left no forwarding address—the day before yesterday."

"I see. Ah, too bad. Well, look, you spoke to her. Was she upset? What's the word, distraught?"

"Distraught? That one? Oh, dear, no," the man said, smiling. "I talked to her while the boy brought her bags down and got her a taxi. Not at all upset. I don't think a woman of her calibre ever shows she's upset, do you, Mr. Dubuque?"

"True. Very true," Dubuque said, nodding profoundly. "Well, thank you. I'm relieved. I can see I shouldn't have been so concerned," but as he left he muttered, "Gone. Gone where? I'll be damned. I'll be goddamned." Outside, standing near his car staring at leaves still wet from the rain and sticking to the pavement, he had to take a deep breath, as if the wind had just been knocked out of him and he had lost all direction. He had to look far up the street to the lighted insurance clock so he could recognize it and get his bearings. An approaching elderly man with a cane stared at him, because, as he concentrated so intently, he seemed to be watching something happening at the big old brick house across the road that had been sandblasted clean and turned into a tavern. Three girls and three men coming out of this tavern had stopped to listen to a long-haired young man who sat on a camp stool playing a guitar and singing, a pail for donations at his feet, his sweet voice coming on the wind. The three girls, deciding to sing with him, tried and tried again, and then, as they laughed hilariously, Dubuque said out loud, "Well, to hell with it. What she wants is what she gets. I'm through." She'd taken up far too much of his time; it was plain he was never going to make a nickel out of her; she was simply too pig-headed to try and realize her potential; and since he had always hated childish men, why should he have any respect for such a childish woman? So he went home.

Being the firm-minded man he was, he let weeks pass without even taking the time to wonder where she had gone. But at breakfast, having his coffee, he would glance quickly through the morning paper just as he used to do, dwelling on any news item about a girl being found dead in a bush or by the roadside or under a bridge. This now was just a habit, something he didn't notice. Ilona wasn't in his mind. Yet by the time the really hot weather came, he found himself becoming bored with his list of housewives willing to service prosperous men. Suddenly he didn't want to bother with them. None of them interested him now. He didn't need them. He dropped them all.

Then, in the middle of September, he felt compelled to go to Mr. Gilhooley's. Gil told him he felt good; he was writing, working late at night. Starting at two in the morning, he sometimes worked till dawn.

"So you've often been in my mind," Gil said. "I've been wanting to ask you—what do you make of the way she came and went?"

Shrugging, Dubuque said, "To tell the truth I never think about her at all."

But as he got around town, eating in expensive restaurants, or going into the big hotels, or shopping with his wife in the little boutiques in the Yorkville area, he would sometimes see a lovely tall girl listening to a worried man, the girl's face suddenly full of compassion and promise, her hand going out to the man—or a man with a worried girl, looking with such soothing concern into her face, his arm going around her waist—and he would think, "Why do I get the feeling Ilona is still around here?"

Seeking him out now, Gil took him to obscure little bars where they could talk and he could question him about his feeling for Ilona. Again and again he told Gil that he had seen her only as a valuable property who could have been a credit to him, a golden whore, and again and again he got from Gil the same wise, indulgent smile. "You poor man," Dubuque said, "you mustn't be childish. I'm sorry for you. You must not try to make the girl into something she wasn't. Half the time I don't know who you're talking about. The sentimentality, it's silly. It's so soft-headed. Look, you didn't know her. I did. You don't really know anything I haven't told you. Do you realize that? So I'll tell you this. Maybe she's dead, but if she isn't dead, wherever she is she's doing the same thing. She's odd around here because she's a natural."

When Gil said, "How do you know?" he said, "For God's sake, Gil, why are you so pig-headed?" When Gil, smiling, looked almost pleased, Dubuque, stiffening, perceived in a flash that Gil wouldn't be offended by anything he said, just interested that he had said it—as a character in his story. Offended, he thought grimly, "It's time I started keeping Mr. Gilhooley away from me."

24

IN LATE SEPTEMBER THERE HAD BEEN A THREE-DAY heat wave, the last of the hot summer days, but Mr. Gilhooley's had been a little oasis just a few steps from the baking street pavements. At five-thirty that afternoon, Gil had been talking to Judge Gibbons, until the Judge looked at his watch and left. Just as he left, the swing door from the lounge was pushed aside as confidently as Dubuque alone used to push it, and into the bar came a portly middle-aged man in an Italian brown-silk suit, the brown cloth minutely flecked with gold, a man with a long face, a prominent nose, and greying black hair combed back smoothly. He looked rich and well-groomed, but in the cut of his clothes and in his air there was something foreign. On his left hand was a gold ring with an emerald in it. First, he stood looking all round the bar with great curiosity, taking it all in without any embarrassment. Then, approaching Gil, he said, "Jeel."

"Jeel?"

"Yes, Jeel."

"Oh, Gil. I'm Gil."

"And this is Mr. Gulhooley's." His English was flawless, but he had a faint accent that seemed to go with his expensive clothes.

"Yeah, Mr. Gilhooley's," Gil said.

"Do you remember a girl, Ilona?"

"Ilona! Do I remember Ilona? Why? Have you seen her? Where did you see her?" Gil asked eagerly.

"About two weeks ago in Montreal," he said, smiling and nodding approval of Gil's eagerness. "And she is well, oh, quite well."

"Have a drink," Gil said. "Let me drink with you. It must be champagne." While he got the drinks, the visitor, now sitting at the bar, kept looking around; he even got up and peered through the lattice. When he had sat down again, Gil, raising a glass to him, said, "In your honor," and he, in turn, raising his glass, said, "My name is Novak. Shipping. My company owns ships, freighters that come up your seaway. I'm here on business. I had a little time. I couldn't resist looking to see if this hotel, this bar, was really here."

"But Ilona. Tell me about Ilona. How did you get to know her?"

"The whole story?"

"The whole story—if you'd be so kind."

"Yes, it gives me pleasure to sit here with Jeel. Ilona did not know you well, but she knew of your interest, and speaks of you often," he said. His face as he talked showed the further pleasure he got watching Gil's eyes. An educated man, he was at ease with his perceptions. He said that in Montreal he had been staying at the Ritz and waiting to meet with an old friend, a Greek named Yamouk, the captain of a Greek freighter that was due to dock in Montreal. He loved this man Yamouk, a big, confident, bearded, laughing man who read a lot. At sea, he said, Yamouk had the time to read and think, so conversation with him was a joy. He hadn't seen Yamouk for six months. When Yamouk's ship docked, he came to the hotel; they sat in the Maritime bar drinking, then Yamouk said firmly, "Now old friend, you are to come and have dinner with me and my wife."

"Your wife!" Novak said. "Where did you pick up a wife?" and he said he had met her in Montreal. She had been staying with some Hungarian relatives; he had met her at a dinner for an exiled Greek political hero. Novak said, "Where do we go for dinner?"

"To our home," he said. And where was that?

"The ship," he said. They lived on the ship. She sailed the seas with him. She was a good sailor, he said.

They drove to the jetty where Yamouk's ship was tied up, boarded it, and were led to the large cabin where a tall girl in an expensive pale-pink sweater and a grey skirt waited, smiling, her hand out. Well, he was mute with surprise, Novak said. Tall and tanned by the sea as she was, and with a face that made him want to catch his breath and forget where he was, she looked like a princess. But Yamouk had patted her playfully on the behind. Though the dinner was served by a steward in a white coat, she explained that she had done the cooking. He asked her if she liked living on the sea. She loved it, she said. She never felt so at home. Going ashore was her excursion time.

"There's a thing I think I'm right about," Novak said. "I've been around long enough to notice some things about men and women who live together. When I go into a home where a man and woman live together, and they are there talking to me, I can tell in half an hour how it is between them. Haven't you noticed this? It's not in what they say. It's an ease. It's in something they make you feel, an intimacy, a smile exchanged, nothing said; the way one listens to the other, a warmth, a closeness they don't even seem to be aware of themselves. I'm sure you've noticed this, Jeel."

Then he went on telling about the amount they drank that night, and how they laughed, and how Yamouk, who was very perceptive, knew that he was expected to talk about Ilona. Teasing her, Yamouk liked it when she teased him back. "I wish you could have seen them," Novak said. "You see, I know about your interest, you and a man named, I think, Dubuque. Is that right? Dubuque? Ah, well, I wish you could see Yamouk leaning back in his chair, his arm across her shoulder, telling me what a great sexy witch she was, and her laughing and pulling at his beard. And he told me, too, that when they're out at sea and he's alone on the bridge, his head is now full of poetry, just as it used to be. Yamouk said this while his hand moved across her neck. 'She takes me across seas I never will really sail,' he says, and they both laugh. Ah, Yamouk is a very smart, earthy man. I could tell he knows where the poetry really is."

"And she talked about this place?" Gil asked.

"Indeed she did," Novak went on. Of course they had been drinking, the talk loosening up, he said. But between her and Yamouk was a remarkable candor, very earthy too, as if they found some magic in their earthiness. While she talked about this hotel and what she did here, Novak said, looking around, he had glanced at Yamouk, wondering when he would tell her to shut up. Then he saw that Yamouk, smiling frankly, really didn't give a damn. "He was more than ever now the master of the world on that ship, maybe even more than a master," he said.

Finishing his drink, Novak said, "Well, I had to see if this place was here. I'm glad I saw it, Jeel, and glad to have met you."

Bewildered by his own elation and wanting to share it, Gil startled Novak by coming out from behind the bar. "Just a minute, please," he said and hurried out of the bar, and out the side door of the hotel, hoping he might catch the Judge still talking to the doorman, but the doorman said the Judge had just got into a taxi. Rushing back to the bar, he found that Mr. Novak, too, had gone. Hazel said he had finished his drink and left the way he had come, through the swing door to the lounge.

As Gil stood at the end of the bar, mute and motionless, the sea in his mind, a stillness came over him. And in the stillness the world's seas seemed to wash around him, which quickened his wonder at what he saw as the rightness of things. Ilona was at home on the sea, at one with the waters, the nurturing waters washing around all human shores, Ilona with her ancient gift, sailing the seas of God.

Then, as the moment passed, and he relaxed, he thought, "What in the world will Dubuque say about this?"